SEASHELLS AND CHRISTMAS BELLS

SHIPWRECK CAFÉ MYSTERIES BOOK #2

DONNA WALO CLANCY

DWC
PUBLISHING

Cover Design: Melissa Ringuette of Monark Design Services
Rogena Mitchell-Jones, Literary Editor
RMJ Manuscript Services www.rogenamitchell.com
Interior Formatting: Rogena Mitchell-Jones

*To all the readers who have stuck it out
with me in my absence from the cozy world.
I thank you immensely.*

*To my mom: I love you more than
you will ever know.*

To my dad: I miss you so much.

*To my sister, Lynne:
You are my biggest cheerleader!*

The warm days of August had turned into the cool days of September. The Shipwreck Café owner and his staff could boast of an extremely successful first summer season.

It was the Monday after Labor Day, and the kids were back in school. The Cape had returned to its slower pace of life, except on weekends. This was the time of year for tour buses and young couples who didn't have children and didn't want to be around them when vacationing.

Jay was enjoying an extra day off, something that hadn't happened all summer. He sat on the picnic table watching his two dogs—Angie, a golden, and Pickles, a black and white Papillon—frolicking at the water's edge. Looking around at the mostly empty parking lot surrounding his privately-owned beach, he was glad the small shack the town employee had sat in all summer while collecting parking fees was now removed for the offseason.

He had vowed this past summer would be the last time the town made money off his property.

When Anchor Point had sat vacant for fifteen years, the town moved in and took over the beach and parking lot areas. They charged over the top fees for tourists to park and use the beach while they were on vacation. When Jay and Robbie were young, their family used this beach all the time, no charge. Jay wanted it to go back the way it was, the way it used to be.

The fact the board of selectmen knew that Jay Hallett now owned all of Anchor Point, and the government had made no effort to even consult with Jay about continuing to use his property, infuriated him. That was all going to change. A registered letter had been sent to the selectmen's office telling them they no longer had permission to use Anchor Point for town use. He was waiting for an answer to the letter delivered to the government official on the first of September.

"Come on, girls," Jay yelled, clapping his hands.

The two dogs stopped what they were doing and looked in Jay's direction.

"Come on. Let's go," Jay repeated.

It had been a long summer, and the dogs hadn't been able to play on the beach with the tourists around. They were not yet ready to leave and went back to playing in the water. Jay laughed, knowing from the moment they arrived it would be difficult to get them to leave once they were there.

"Hey, Jay," Robbie called from behind him.

Robbie Hallett, Jay's younger brother, was a surfer. Whenever he wasn't bartending at the café, he was riding the waves on his favorite board. He lived in the smaller cottage behind the keeper's house where Jay and the dogs lived.

"Nice waves out there today," Jay replied.

"The liquor order is done, and I am spending the day in the sun," Robbie said as he smiled broadly. "I didn't get as much of a tan as I usually do. I worked more this summer than I ever have before, but my bank account balance is the biggest it's ever been to get through the winter months."

"You'll still be working through the winter, but things have really slowed down so there will be plenty of time to surf now," Jay said, turning his attention to the dogs who had moved further up the beach. "We'll get busy around the holidays again."

"What are they doing?" Robbie asked, following Jay's gaze.

"I think Colleen, the ghost, is calling them," Jay admitted. "She must want to play."

"Another ghost that you haven't told me about?" Robbie sighed.

"Colleen O'Mara was a ten-year-old girl who drowned when *The Fallen Mist* crashed on the point in the nor'easter at the turn of the century. Her body washed ashore, but her mother's body was never found. Her ghost roams the point calling out for her mother," Jay answered.

"That's sad," Robbie replied.

"I asked Roland about it, but he said he looked for days and never found the mother's body," Jay stated.

"Roland would know. He was there, after all," Robbie said, setting his board down and taking his shirt off.

Roland Knowles, another resident ghost, was the lighthouse keeper at the turn of the century. He was murdered in 1910 for a pirate treasure that he had found and hidden again. He wouldn't give up the location and died protecting the information. Most of his time was spent up in the lighthouse looking out over the point.

"I was actually coming to get you," Robbie said, picking up his board and strapping on the ankle guard. "The contractors are waiting for you to verify the spot where Mom's cottage is going to be built."

"I forgot they were coming today," Jay said, standing up and calling for the dogs.

This time, Angie and Pickles responded to Jay's calls and ran to their owner. They had to wait for Pickles to catch up as her little legs couldn't keep up with Angie's. Leaving the beach, they headed up the road to home. After setting down treats and fresh water, Jay left to meet the contractor.

Bill Swann had done all the work on the café before its opening. Jay admired his work and his dedication to completing the job on schedule. He insisted that they could have Martha, Jay's mom, in her new home before Christmas. She was staying in the spare room at Jay's cottage as she had sold her house to move to Florida, but her plans to move had been canceled.

"Bill, good to see you again," Jay said.

"You, too. I hear you had a really good first season," Bill replied, shaking the hand that had been extended by Jay. "Ghosts and all."

"We had a great summer season. Roland made his presence known here and there, scaring the daylights out of my customers." Jay chuckled.

"I knew something was funny when my tools kept disappearing in the café," Bill stated.

"You won't have to worry about him out here on the back end of the point. He pretty much stays in the lighthouse," Jay informed. "He doesn't like noise."

"I talked to Martha and showed her the plans for the cottage. They had everything she requested included, and she signed off on them. I just need to know if where the orange stakes are laid out is where the house is going to be built."

"Yes, it is. My mom wants her bay window in the living room to look out over the ocean. I think she is counting on Roland to come visit her and wants to afford him an ocean view," Jay admitted.

"Your mom is a hoot. Leave it up to her to want a ghost as a friend." Bill laughed.

"I know... she is unique." Jay smiled.

"We will be up here to break ground on next Monday. The foundation should be poured by Thursday," Bill announced.

"Great. I'll tell her what's happening."

"Jay, can I give you a piece of advice?" Bill asked.

"Sure. Is there something wrong with my mom's house plans?"

"No, this is more serious. Word around town is that you sent a letter to the selectmen telling them the town can no longer use the point for beach parking and collecting fees. Is that true?"

"That was a private letter sent to the board. How the heck did that get around town already?" Jay asked, frustrated.

"I know you moved away for a while, but some things never change. Nothing is a secret around here. Everyone knows everyone's business, including town business," Bill said. "So, it's true?"

"Yes, it is. I want my beach and parking lot to be a first come, first serve and free to the families that come here on vacation. My family never paid a cent to enjoy the beach, and I want it to be that way again," Jay answered.

"Just so you know, there are quite a few people who are not happy with the loss of income that will occur in the town's revenue without the beach fees."

"It doesn't matter who will be happy or who won't be. It's my private property, and I will do what I see fit with it," Jay insisted.

"I'm just warning you to be careful. My brother Sid has been a selectman for a very long time and is used to getting what he wants. And he wants to continue to collect those fees."

"I can handle Sid Swann," Jay said. "Legally, he doesn't have a leg to stand on."

"Okay, well, I guess I will see you Monday," he replied.

He watched Bill hop up in his truck and drive away. Jay had to remember he was back home, and Anchor Point still had a small-town mentality. He hoped Sid wouldn't cause too much trouble over Jay's decision, but his mind was made up, and nothing would change it.

2

"Hey, boss, what are you doing here? This is your day off," Susan yelled from behind the steamer. "Go work on a late-season tan or something."

"I have some things to check on for the Seashells and Christmas Bells Ball that we're holding here. It's still three months away, but that time will pass by fast."

"I think it's a great idea to want to reserve the Tunnel of Ships and open it to the public as a museum. History is so interesting," Susan replied. "I am sure you will sell lots of tickets to benefit the project."

"That's a great name—Tunnel of Ships. Do you mind if I use that?" Jay requested.

"I'd be honored," Susan replied.

"Although it's not really the ships that are down there but items off the crashed ships. I'll have to run that by Roland and see if he approves." Jay smiled, stealing a cup of his mother's famous chowder for lunch.

"The seashell tree is a great idea, too. Lots of kids will benefit when a shell is plucked off the tree for them. Seashell Friends was genius!"

"I'm going to put a huge tree up in the lobby on November first. People can begin to participate once we get the shells hung on there,"

Jay informed her. "All the gifts will have to be returned to under the tree, labeled with the child's name by the night of the ball."

"Do you think that you'll make enough money from the ticket sales to complete the tunnel project?"

"I hope so, but I am not so sure now."

"Why? Everyone loves this place and the food you serve. Why wouldn't it be a successful fund raiser?" Susan was puzzled.

"It appears I am not a very popular person in town right now. I sent the letter I showed you to the selectmen telling them they can't use my property anymore. Word has leaked out about it thanks to Sid Swann."

"You know how small towns are. Nothing says secret for long." Susan sighed.

"I was thinking of donating the museum entrance fees to the town in place of the beach fees, but now I am having seconds thoughts on that, too."

"Personally, I think you are worrying for nothing. The event will be a total success."

"I hope you're right. I also have the reading of Mr. Peterson's will this month, which isn't going to earn me any brownie points with two locals and their families," Jay stated.

Mr. Peterson, an elderly friend of his mother's, had died during the summer. Before that, his two kids committed him to an assisted living facility off-Cape and had abandoned his dog to the streets. The golden stayed at the lighthouse, the last place where she had seen her loving owner.

When Jay bought the property, he fell in love with the dog and took her in. They had been best friends ever since. While seeking help in a previous mystery, Jay brought the dog for a ride when he went to see Mr. Peterson, who immediately recognized his beloved pet. Realizing his children had abandoned her, he cut them out of his will.

Jay was made executor and all the money was left to him to use at his discretion to help animals. Peterson's two kids promised to fight the new will right up to the highest court. Jay had no idea what he had gotten mixed up in, but he would soon find out at the reading of the will.

"They shouldn't have been such jerks in the first place, abandoning such a beautiful dog the way they did. They deserve to lose everything in favor of the animals," Susan insisted. "You know the law. I wouldn't worry about that too much, either."

"I know, but..." Jay hesitated.

"You have to remember you are back in a small town. Things blow over as quick as they blow up. Stop worrying," Susan admonished.

"I hope you're right. I'll be in my office."

Jay settled in behind his desk. There were bills to pay and schedules to complete. He had also been collecting Christmas catalogs to peruse so he could start ordering items needed to decorate the café for the holidays and the upcoming festivities. His mother had offered to help in the decorating process and had quite a few of the catalogs at the cottage.

Much quieter now...

Jay turned to see Roland hovering in the far corner of the office.

"Yes, it is, my friend. I haven't seen you around for a while. What have you been up to?"

Visiting with Martha.

"My mom loves your visits. I need to ask you something," Jay said, standing up and stretching.

Roland floated over to the window. He seemed anxious about something.

What is it that you need to ask?

"I would like your permission to turn the tunnel under the café into a museum. I want to enclose all the shelves you dug out of the dirt walls behind glass to preserve the items off the shipwrecks. Susan suggested it be called 'The Tunnel of Ships,' but I told her I would have to run it by you."

I like that...Tunnel of Ships.

"Of course, I will need your help in gathering information on the various ships and items that washed ashore after the shipwrecks," Jay stated. "I want it to be a memorial where visitors can pay homage to those lost out on Anchor Point. Will you help me?"

I will help you...if you help me.

"What do you need, Roland? You know that I will do anything I can…"

Roland looked out the window, sighed and vanished before Jay could finish his sentence.

I wonder what that was all about. What kind of help can a ghost need? Jay walked to the window where Roland had been standing.

Out on the point, Jay could just barely make out the ghostly image of Colleen. She stood looking out over the ocean searching for her mother. Jay knew that Roland still felt guilty, even in the afterlife, that he never found the body of the young girl's mother after the storm.

Maybe it has something to do with Colleen.

Jay finished his paperwork, said goodbye to Susan in the kitchen and left for home. He planned to spend the night going over the will and legal papers of George Peterson before he had to go to the attorney's office the following Saturday. Although he wasn't actively using his law degree, it did come in handy at times when having to read and understand legal documents.

Angie and Pickles met him at the door, tails wagging. The house was quiet. Martha was at the café cooking her well-known chowder. Business had slowed down enough that she only worked every other day or every third day. On her time off, she would visit the hair salon where she used to be a receptionist to catch up on town gossip. Several nights a week she would play bingo with her group of lady friends. Her life had pretty much returned to normal after deciding not to move to Florida.

Jay grabbed a beer out of the refrigerator, then gathered the legal documents he needed to read and headed to the living room with the two dogs in tow. After starting a fire, he sat on the leather couch surrounded by his furry roommates, making notes of legal avenues to fight the family members who were cut from the will.

He was deeply engrossed in the will when a rock came crashing through his front window. The dogs jumped off the couch, barking wildly while running for the front door. Jay flew off the couch and flung open the door. He followed the dogs who ran toward the road that led down off the point.

Jay could see all the way down to the main road, and no cars were traveling away from the direction of the keeper's cottage. He looked over the surrounding area to see if he could spot anyone on foot. Seeing nothing, he called the dogs and returned to the house.

Gating the dogs in the kitchen, he put on a pair of rubber gloves and picked up the rock. He untied the twine and spread out the paper that enclosed the rock. In bold, black letters, centered in the middle of the paper was a warning.

GO BACK TO THE CITY

Jay pulled out his cell phone and called his friend Chief Stephen Boyd.

3

"I have to hire you a full-time bodyguard," Boyd joked as he looked at the broken window. "Seriously, any idea who it was or why?"

Stephen Boyd was close to Jay's family. He grew up in Anchor Point and raised from the rank of patrolman to chief in record time. Liked by all, his intuition and good judgment made him a great asset to the local police department.

"I have a couple of ideas, but no proof," Jay replied. "This is what broke the window."

Jay handed the rock and the note over to Boyd, which he had slipped into a plastic bag.

"Did you handle this at all?"

"No, I was hoping you could check for fingerprints. I used gloves to put it in the bag," Jay answered.

"Good. I'll take this to the lab boys and see if they can come up with anything. Now, tell me, who do you think could be responsible for this?"

Jay told him about who he suspected the most and why. Sid Swann and Greg Peterson's family members were the names on the top of his list.

"I won't question them until we see if we can lift some prints off the rock or the note. I'll be in touch when I know anything," he stated. "Be careful."

Boyd left with the evidence, and Jay found some cardboard to close off where the window used to be. He placed a call to have it repaired, and they promised to be there first thing in the morning. The dogs were jumping on the gate trying to get out of the kitchen. Satisfied that all the glass had been swept up, Jay released the dogs. They ran to the front door, whining.

Ten seconds later, his mom walked in.

"What happened?" Martha asked, staring at the cardboard place holder.

Jay told his mom what happened and admonished her to be careful until they knew who it was that lobbed the rock through the window.

"Honestly, Jay. You get yourself into more trouble," Martha said, rolling her eyes and heading for the kitchen. "Are you going to be here for supper?"

"I was planning on it," he replied, following her.

"How's swordfish sound?" His mother smiled, holding up a plastic bag. "I snagged this from the fish delivery that came in today. One of the perks of being the owner's mother!"

"Sounds good to me. I will be reading George Peterson's legal documents tonight. Crap..." he muttered as he left the kitchen.

Jay ran to the living room where he had left the legal documents. They were gone. He dug his phone out of his pocket and called Boyd.

"That's right. Whoever threw the rock must have come into the house while I was out with the dogs looking for them."

"That was kind of stupid. It points the blame right in the direction of the Peterson kids," the chief stated. "I'll look into it. Say hi to Martha for me."

"Seriously, they were in the house?" Martha asked. "Do you think it was one of the Peterson kids?"

Not the Petersons... older man. The ghost was standing next to the whalebone mantel, admiring his handiwork.

"Have you seen him before, Roland? Maybe at the café?"

No... never.

"Thank you, Roland. At least now we know it was an older man. I'll call Boyd back and let him know."

Welcome... Bye, Martha.

Roland shimmered out, and Martha returned to the kitchen to start supper. Jay called the chief back for the third time and told him what Roland had said. If the chief hadn't seen Roland for himself, he would have taken what Jay was telling him with a grain of salt. But the ghost had been such a tremendous help in catching Bea's killer, the chief couldn't ignore anything Roland said.

Jay's next call was to George Peterson's attorney who promised to overnight copies of all the documents that had been taken. He also informed Jay that he had already had several contentious meetings with the Peterson's attorney, and George's kids weren't going to go down without a fight. The attorney ended the call by telling Jay he would see him Saturday morning.

Martha and her son enjoyed a quiet dinner together. Much of their discussion centered on the Christmas Ball that was going to be held at the café the second week of December. They perused the catalogs that Martha had brought home from the café while they ate and chose items to be ordered that fit the theme—seashells and Christmas bells.

Jay also needed to order a hundred four-inch plastic scallop shells to be hung on the big tree in the front lobby near the door. They would write numbers in red marker on the inside of the shell and place them on the tree. Each number would correspond to a list containing the name of a child or family who needed help at Christmas.

The list would be locked in Jay's office so the names of the donors and the names of the people receiving the gifts would remain anonymous, known only to Jay, Robbie, Martha, or Kathy, the head hostess.

"We have accomplished quite a bit tonight," Martha said, collecting the dishes off the table. "I'm going to put the dishes in the dishwasher and go to bed."

"I'll clean up. Go ahead to bed," Jay offered.

"Okay, if you insist. See you in the morning."

Jay watched his mom walk away. His mind wandered back to a couple of months ago when he thought he had lost her. He never realized just how much she meant to him until she was almost gone. He vowed at that point to spend as much time as possible with her and to give her the best life he could. She deserved it.

Dishes finished, he grabbed a beer out of the refrigerator and went to sit in front of the fireplace with his dogs. Staring into the flames, he thought about Roland's treasure for the first time in months. The ghost insisted that it would never be found, and Jay took that as a challenge to find it.

Roland's journal has confiscated as evidence in Bea Thomas's murder trial, but at the trial's conclusion, Jay would get it back. Jay had made copies of every page before he turned it over to the police, and he kept the small key and a piece of paper he found hidden in the front cover of the journal.

Once the holidays were over, Jay would have lots of extra time on his hands to look for the treasure. By then, he should have the original journal back from the police.

The one item Jay never relinquished or reminded anyone he had was Roland's gold pocket watch. The front of the watch pictured the ship, *The Fallen Mist*, in raised detail. The back had the ship's name and the date of the crash the ship was destroyed out on the point. It was forged out of melted gold that was part of the pirate treasure Roland had found. Roland always carried the watch with him as a reminder that he was responsible for the ship crashing the night of the storm. The light had gone out in the lighthouse, and he couldn't get it lit again because of the fierce winds. He tried repeatedly but failed. In his heart, he felt he had caused the deaths of all those aboard the ship because there was no light to guide them away from the rocky shore of the point.

The watch had been placed in Jay's safe. No one had asked about it, and he didn't offer any information on it. He wasn't going to let it out of his possession as Roland had told him that it held the key to the location of the treasure.

He finished his beer and shooed the dogs off the couch. Pulling out the sofa bed, he decided to sleep on the first floor because of the missing window. The dogs were already on the bed and asleep by the time he got back from the bathroom. He crawled under the sheets, staying to one side so as not to disturb his furry roommates.

4

The next day, Martha had agreed to stay at the cottage until the window was fixed. Jay left for work as he needed to enter the payroll into the computer as well as the following week's schedule. Plans had been made to join Cindy at the Burger Box for lunch, and all the paperwork had to be finished before Jay could leave for his lunch date.

Cindy Nickerson was Jay's girlfriend in high school. He broke up with her when he left for college and law school. He never forgot about her, and they rekindled their relationship when he moved back home. They agreed to take things slow, but so far, Jay hadn't dated anyone else since his return.

"Jay, you just got an overnight delivery package. I signed for it," Kathy said, setting it on his desk.

"Thanks. It must be the replacement papers that were stolen from my house last night," Jay stated, reaching for the envelope.

"I heard about that. The dogs weren't hurt, were they?"

"They're fine."

"Before you ask...I heard about it at the coffee shop this morning," Kathy said. "I also heard that Sid Swann is not a happy camper right now. None of the selectmen are either since they received your letter."

"Such privacy…" Jay mumbled.

"No such thing in this town," Kathy retorted, going out the door.

Martha was home with the dogs so Jay could leave the café directly for town and his lunch date. Cindy motioned for him to sit in the corner booth near the front window. Minutes later, she had shed her apron and joined him.

The Burger Box was a popular place. Good food and reasonable prices. The fact that it stayed open year-round made it the place to go for lunch. Today was no exception as the place was packed. As the couple sat enjoying their seafood chowder and BLTs, Sid Swann appeared at the end of their booth.

"Hello, Sid," Jay said, looking up from his lunch.

"Are you really going to go through with this?" he demanded in a loud voice.

"Sid, this is not the time or the place to discuss this. I received your letter for the meeting between myself and the selectmen, and I will talk to you then," Jay answered.

"No! We will discuss it now," he insisted.

By this time, all eyes were on the two men arguing in the corner of the restaurant.

"Your brother told me that you were used to getting your way. Selectman or not, I don't answer to anyone. You want to get into this in front of everyone here, fine," Jay said, standing up. "It is my land and my beach, and I can do with it what I see fit. You mooched off the land for the last fifteen years without permission from the previous owner, but I won't be such a pushover."

"You do realize we can take the land from you by eminent domain?" Sid asked, red in the face.

"You can try, but you don't have a legal leg to stand on. When the judge finds out how you treated the previous owner and how you didn't even ask my permission to use privately-owned land this year, you will get laughed out of court," Jay stated.

"You think just because you returned to Anchor Point as a wealthy attorney that you are better than the rest of us," Sid fumed. "You are taking town revenue out of our meager budget, and it won't sit well with the locals—the working locals who can't afford to have their taxes increased to cover the loss."

"I think you should leave now, Sid," Jay stated in a firm voice.

"What? You don't want people to know what kind of person you really are?" Sid yelled.

"You want them to know who I really am? I am opening a new museum on the point, and I was going to donate the new museum entrance fees to the town to make up for the loss of revenue. But you just made up my mind not to do that either. Get out of here, Sid, before I do something I may regret," Jay warned.

"Is that a threat?" Sid asked, making sure everyone in the restaurant had heard Jay's last statement.

"Take it as you see fit," he mumbled, sitting down again.

"You heard him, everyone. Be careful of this person. He isn't the nice guy he seems to be. He's taking food out of your family's mouths and hurting the town he calls home," Sid announced.

"It seems to me that you are the one hurting this town, Sid. You wouldn't have had a loss of income if you had just shut up and left like you were asked to do," Cindy said loudly. "Now leave my restaurant before I call the police and have you arrested for disturbing the peace!"

"You'll be sorry you messed with me, *Mr. Hallett*," Sid warned as he slammed his way out the door.

The place was as quiet as a tomb. All eyes were on Jay.

"I'm sorry, Cindy, but I have lost my appetite. Can we make this another day?" Jay requested.

"Sure," she offered. "Things will blow over. Sid thinks he owns this town and that what he says goes. He's not used to anyone going against what he wants."

"I'll call you later," he said, standing up.

As he left the Burger Box, people were whispering behind his back and looking away. He'd get even with Sid somehow. Maybe he would run against him for his spot as selectman next election. No, Jay didn't want anything to do with politics. He was just mad and not thinking straight. But he did wonder just how fast Sid could spread this little episode around town, as it would definitely hurt the ticket sales for the Christmas Ball.

5

*J*ay returned home. Martha was nowhere to be found, and Jay assumed she was at the hair salon getting her daily dose of gossip. He let Angie and Pickles out the back door and sat on the deck watching them while drinking a beer.

He sat back and closed his eyes. The September sun felt warm on his face, and he was finally starting to relax after his run-in with Sid. The dogs started barking. Jay opened his eyes to see what they were going on about.

A petite woman in jeans and a sweater stood at the edge of the deck. Jay figured her to be in her mid-fifties. She was wearing sunglasses, which Jay could see were hiding a black eye and a bruised cheek.

"Mr. Jeremy Hallett?" she asked meekly.

"Yes, but people around here call me Jay," he answered standing up.

As he walked closer, he saw bruises on her arms and wrists peeking out from under the sleeves of her sweater. When she saw him looking at them, she pulled her sleeves down to hide them. She stood there quietly as if planning what she wanted to say before she said it.

"What can I help you with?" he asked when she remained quiet.

"I'm here to warn you. Please don't make Sid mad. You have no idea what he is capable of doing," she whispered, head down.

"Who are you?" Jay inquired.

"That's not important. Just be careful if you intend to go forward with your plans to defy Sid Swann."

"Did he do that to you?" Jay asked, pointing to her eye.

"I shouldn't have come here. Please, never tell anyone that I spoke to you."

She ran off not looking back. Jay watched her climb into an older model Mustang. He was too far away to get a plate number, but there couldn't be that many older Mustangs in the area. He would have to run it by Boyd when he got a chance.

"Come on, girls. I need to go to the café," Jay yelled. The dogs had moved further out on the point playing with Colleen the ghost. She looked up and vanished, and the dogs pranced back to the deck.

He strolled leisurely to the café. How was he going to undo the damage that Sid had done to his reputation? His mother had always said to turn the other cheek, but working in Boston, Jay learned that wasn't always possible. Some people had to be dealt with directly and forcibly. Sid Swann was one of those people.

Jay had forgotten to take home the packet of papers he received in the mail. Tonight would be the last free time he would have to scan the documents as he had to work the night shift on Friday. Saturday morning, he had to be at the attorney's office at ten.

"Hey, boss. We got shorted on our produce delivery again today. This makes four times in a row," Susan complained. "Can you give the company a call?"

"I'll take care of it," Jay mumbled as he walked through the kitchen.

He grabbed the papers and ducked out the back door near the lighthouse. Jay wasn't in the mood to deal with people right now, especially the owner of Fresh Produce, Inc. He had several conversations with him over the summer about lost produce that never seemed to make it off the truck and into the café. Things seemed to be going well, but now, the problems were starting up again. Jay would call him on Monday.

"Jay, is that you?" his mother yelled as he entered through the back door.

"It's me, Mom."

"I'm going out with Theresa. You are on your own cooking tonight," Martha yelled from her first-floor bedroom. "I'll be home after bingo."

"Have a good time and win big," he said, feeding the dogs their supper.

Martha left by the front door. Jay still wasn't hungry. He grabbed a new flavor beer that a beer rep had left for Robbie and him to try so maybe they would carry the line at the café bar. He settled on the couch in front of a newly lit fire and started to read.

The dogs had full bellies and went to sleep on their doggie pillows that were in front of the fireplace. Perusing the will and the other legal documents, Jay saw no loopholes or problems with carrying out the last wishes of Mr. Peterson. He was confident that the elderly man's two children had no way to win or nullify their father's latest will.

Problems?

"Roland, I didn't hear you come in," Jay said, setting down the papers he was holding. "Well, that was stupid. Of course, I wouldn't hear you come in."

Problems?

"Just a few, my friend," Jay answered, shaking his head.

Before Roland could respond, a knock sounded on the door. The ghost shimmered out, and Jay went to open the front door. A serious looking Chief Boyd entered the house.

"Stephen, I was going to call you tomorrow," Jay said, smiling at his friend.

"This is not a social call, Jay. Where have you been tonight, since, say, seven o'clock?"

"I've been here going over legal papers for a meeting I have Saturday morning. Why?"

"Can anyone vouch for you?"

"Only the dogs," Jay chuckled. "And Roland."

"This is serious, my friend. Sid Swann was murdered tonight. He was working late at the town hall, and someone got him in the back with a letter opener. His secretary left at five o'clock and claims that Sid was alive and elbow deep in paperwork when she went home."

"Sid's dead?" Jay repeated. "Why would you want to know where I was tonight? Do you think that I had something to do with his murder?"

"People heard the fight between you two at the Burger Box earlier today. Several witnesses said that you threatened him."

"I did. But it was just to get him to leave the restaurant," Jay insisted. "Not to kill him."

"Don't leave Anchor Point. We are still collecting evidence, and you are not in the clear yet. You probably know the law better than anyone around here. Your threat makes you our number one suspect."

"Come on, Stephen. You know I didn't kill Sid. Yeah, we had words, but that's all it was—words," Jay stated. "How did you find out Sid was dead?"

"We got an anonymous phone call at the station."

"How convenient. The caller is probably your killer," Jay stated.

"I'm serious. Don't plan any trips until this is cleared up."

"I have an attorney's appointment for the reading of a will off-Cape on Saturday morning that I can't miss. It's at ten o'clock, and I should return no later than noon."

"Give me the attorney's name and phone number so that I can verify the meeting," Boyd replied.

Jay wrote the information on a loose piece of paper that was on the coffee table. He held up the will to show the chief. Boyd looked at the front page for the name of the office to compare it to the information given to him.

"George Peterson's will. I hear the talk going around town about how his kids are challenging the latest will. Good luck with this one," he said, handing the scrap of paper back to Jay. "I don't need this now."

"Thanks for trusting me," Jay replied.

"Just don't give me cause to have to come up here again. Be home on Saturday like you said you would be," the sheriff admonished.

Martha came through the front door, home from bingo. She waved a stack of bills around in the air, smiling broadly.

"I won five hundred dollars." She beamed. "I got the last jackpot of the night."

"That's wonderful, Martha," Boyd replied.

It was then that Martha felt the tenseness in the air.

"What's going on?" she asked.

"Sid Swann was murdered tonight, and I am the number one suspect because I threatened him at lunch today," Jay stated, frowning.

"Sid's dead? God forgive me, but it couldn't have happened to a nicer person," Martha said, taking off her coat.

"Mom!"

"What? I'm only saying out loud what half the town will be thinking tomorrow when word gets out."

"Unfortunately, your mom's right. He wasn't very well liked around here."

"No, he wasn't. He was an arrogant, pushy individual who would sell out his own mother to get his way," Martha stated. "And his poor wife…"

"What about his wife, Mom?" Jay inquired.

"He would beat that poor woman for no reason at all, but she would never press charges against him. He had some kind of hold on her, and no one could figure out what it was."

"Is she a petite woman, mid-fifties?" Jay asked.

"Yes, why?" Boyd asked.

Jay told them about the woman who came to warn him that afternoon out on the deck. The woman was covered in bruises and had a black eye. He told the sheriff it was why he was going to be calling him. The woman drove an early Mustang, and he wanted to find out who she was.

"That sounds like Emmaline Swann. She drives a Mustang," Boyd confirmed.

"Have you asked her where she was tonight? Maybe she finally snapped and whacked her husband herself," Jay stated.

"We did, and she was home alone. No one can vouch for her, either," Boyd answered.

"Either? Stephen, use your common sense. You must know that my son couldn't kill anyone. I can name a dozen people who would have loved to see him dead. Do you want a list?" Martha snapped.

"Unfortunately, Martha, we are compiling such a list now... and it's not a short one.

"I'm going to bed. I have to be up early to make chowder for the weekend," Martha said, heading for her bedroom. "Goodnight, Stephen."

"Don't be mad at me, Martha. I am just doing my job."

She didn't answer and closed the door to her room.

He was here all night...

"Thank you, Roland," Boyd said, turning to face the ghost. "But unfortunately, I can't use a ghost as a witness."

6

The next morning, Jay let the dogs out and walked to the end of the driveway to pick up his newspaper. The front page featured a picture of Sid Swann at his last swearing-in as selectman with the caption One Last Time.

The article went on to list all of Sid's achievements while he sat on the board for Anchor Point. It also described the fight between Jay and Sid the previous day at the Burger Box.

This is not good.

Jay tucked the paper under his arm and called the girls into the house. Martha was just coming out of her room and saw the worried look on her son's face.

"What's going on?" she asked, pouring herself a cup of coffee.

He tossed the paper on the kitchen table. She glanced at it and frowned.

"Don't worry. Stephen will find the real killer, and you'll be cleared," she stated.

"This article makes me look really bad. The worst part is, today is the first day the tickets to the Christmas Ball are going on sale. How many do you think we'll sell when people read this?"

"It's only September, and the event is still a long way off. You'll be cleared by then. I can feel it in my bones. Don't worry," Martha insisted. "I have to run. I need to have the first batch of chowder done before lunch, or there won't be any for the noon special."

"I'll be over later," Jay said. "I work the night shift tonight."

He sat at the table turning his coffee cup in a circle. It was not that he didn't trust Chief Boyd to find the murderer, he was a really good cop, but Jay felt like he was already found guilty by the locals, judging by the newspaper article.

"Well, I know I didn't do it," Jay said to the dogs curled up at his feet waiting for their breakfast. "I have to keep going with my normal routine or people will say I am trying to hide something."

He fed the dogs and left for the pier. Every Friday morning, he would go down to the boats and order his fish for the coming weekend. Jay enjoyed the walk through the center of town and his stop at the local coffee shop.

When he reached the pier, the boats were just coming in on the high tide. The ones already docked were off-loading their catches into large, ice-filled metal containers. He looked over the various boats' catches and walked to the fish market.

A retired fisherman named Cappy owned the market. He was a crusty old goat who loved to give everyone who came into his shop a little grief. A newcomer to the shop would be afraid of him because of his gruff manner and his sick sense of humor. He walked around the market with a filet knife in one hand and a pipe in the other. Once you got to know him, you found out he was nothing but a big teddy bear, especially when it came to children.

Jay walked around checking out the various cases holding the freshly caught fish from the pier. Standing in line at the counter waiting his turn, he could see several people covering their mouths in whispers while staring at him. He knew what they were saying, and it made him mad that he was being assumed guilty of murder because of a stupid argument in the diner. The newspaper article hadn't helped his cause, either.

"Jay, how you been, son?" Cappy greeted him with a firm handshake and a smile when it was his turn at the counter.

"Things have been better," Jay answered truthfully.

"I heard. People around here have to gossip," Cappy said, watching the same two people Jay had been watching. "They forget in this country you are innocent until proven guilty."

"I didn't do it," Jay insisted.

"I know you didn't. Don't worry, the truth will come out," Cappy said, raising his voice so that everyone in the market could hear him. "Then, they'll be a whole lot of people around here who owe you a big apology."

"Thanks, Cappy. I needed to hear that from someone besides a family member," Jay stated. "How about I place a big order of the freshest fish available on Cape Cod for my café?"

While the two men figured out Jay's fish order, several locals came up to him and patted him on the back assuring him that not everyone in town felt the same way others did. Jay left the market feeling reenergized and having a little more faith in the town's people than he had before he left his house that morning.

Chief Boyd pulled up in his truck, adjacent to Jay.

"Hop in," he yelled out the window. "I have some things I need to tell you."

Jay jumped in the passenger's side while the cars behind the sheriff beeped at the delay.

"Where are you heading?"

"I'm on my home," Jay answered, jumping up into the cab of the truck. "So, what is it you have to tell me?"

"Your fingerprints weren't on the weapon used in Sid Swann's murder. Two sets of prints came back on the letter opener. His secretary's and another set that we ran through IAFIS and turned up no hits."

"I could have worn gloves, you know," Jay replied.

"I'm trying to help you out here," Boyd said, giving him a puzzling look.

"I'm joking, Stephen."

"This is not something to joke about," Boyd warned. "Half the town thinks you're guilty."

"I know, especially after that front-page story in the paper this morning," Jay replied.

"Are you going to sue them?"

"No, but I would like a retraction printed," Jay said.

The chief turned his truck up the dirt road that led to the lighthouse. He slowed down, looking upwards.

"I wonder how many people can see Roland standing up there keeping watch?"

"Not too many, hopefully. This place would be a real circus. I've already had four groups of paranormal investigators ask for permission to come and poke around the place at night," Jay said, looking up at Roland.

"You turned them down, I assume?"

"Yes, I did. I look at it this way—it would be an invasion of Roland's privacy."

"I guess you're right. He might get a little testy with strangers being here during his quiet time at night."

"Did Sid work late at night a lot?" Jay asked.

"According to his secretary, he did."

"Can you release the fact that my fingerprints weren't on the letter opener and that someone else's was? Someone unknown," Jay asked. "It would really help my situation with the locals."

"I have an appointment with some new reporter from the paper this afternoon. I will make sure I mention it in my statement," Boyd assured him.

He stopped in front of the café.

"Keep me updated, will you, Stephen?" Jay asked, exiting the truck.

"I will. Say hi to Martha for me."

"Will do," he said, waving as he entered the café door.

Lunch was in full swing. A touring company from Maine had called Jay earlier in the week to see if their busload of travelers could eat lunch at the café. Fifty-two people were chatting and eating lunch along with a smattering of locals. Jay looked around, frowning.

I hope the locals come back after Chief Boyd releases his information this afternoon.

Kathy, the head hostess, walked up with a pile of menus she had collected from the tables. She placed them in their slots and turned to Jay.

"The contractor will be here at two to go into the tunnel and take some measurements for the plexiglass walls. He requested that you be here to answer any questions that he has," Kathy stated.

"Thanks for the reminder. I was going to draw some lines in the dirt for him to follow. I guess I will go do it now," Jay replied. "Are you okay here?"

"We're fine. I know where to find you if I need you."

"You're the best." Jay smiled. "I don't know what I would do without you."

"A raise might help you not to have to find out." She chuckled.

"I just gave you a raise in August."

"Can't blame a girl for trying," Kathy replied, walking off to greet new patrons coming in the door.

Jay entered the kitchen. Susan was on the front line, and everything was running smoothly. Although Jay was sorry Ty had been murdered, he was glad Susan was here to step up and take over as First Executive Chef. The other workers in the kitchen loved her as she was fair and understanding, but she still could be a bear when it came to the kitchen running at its best.

"Hey, boss," Susan yelled over the clattering pans and dishes.

He waved and kept going to the cellar door. Turning on all the lights so he could see into the first part of the tunnel, he lit a battery-operated lantern to use once the cellar light faded.

He slid open the two secret doors and proceeded to the main area of the now named Tunnel of Ships. Deciding the door at the other end of the tunnel would throw more light to work by, he walked to the opposite end and opened it. Sunlight flooded the long tunnel, enough that Jay could shut off the lantern.

When Roland was alive and was the lighthouse caretaker, he was very much attached to the people who lost their lives in the shipwrecks along the point. Great care had been taken with each item, and a small slip of paper was placed next to it with the name of the ship the item had come from. Over time, the pieces of paper had started to disintegrate, and some were barely legible because of faded ink.

I sure hope Roland can remember the story behind each of these items.

He stood looking at the artifacts that had been placed into the dug-out holes in the dirt walls. There were combs and brushes, teacups, smoking pipes, and many other personal items from the wrecks. Lanterns that probably swung on the decks of the ships lined the floor, each bearing a tag with a ship's name. Maps, journals, and manifests were also included in the historical treasures.

Planks of wood from the smashed ships were used as dividers between the individual items. There were several splintered sections of masts lying around on the floor. Standing in the corner by itself was a small, unmarked anchor.

So sad...

"Yes, it is, Roland. But we are going to let people see this and pay their respects to those people who were lost," Jay replied. "All your work will be preserved behind protective glass, and we will work together to provide the visitors as much information as we can about the people and the ships that you have memorialized here."

People will come to see this?

"Yes, they will. It is a part of history, and you have made it available to the new generations through your actions over one hundred years ago," Jay replied as he looked at the ghost.

I will help...

The ghost faded away, leaving Jay alone in the tunnel. He walked from hole to hole reading the names of the ships. He made a mental note to bring a notebook with him next time he came down to write the ship's names for further research.

Next, he started to draw lines in the dirt for the contractor. The frame would be three feet out from the wall and in eight-foot sections. A wooden table set at a forty-five-degree slant would be just to the outside of each section giving the history of what was included in that space.

As Jay dragged his heel along in the dirt, it caught on something buried just underneath the surface. He knelt and started to carefully displace the dirt from around the buried item. After a few minutes, he uncovered an emerald-encrusted hair comb. It was all intact. Jay sat down to clean the dirt from in between the crevices of the emeralds.

A muffled sobbing could be heard from where he was sitting. At first, he thought it had to be Roland, but it sounded more like a woman crying. He sat quietly trying to figure out exactly where it was coming from, but the longer it went on, the more it seemed to engulf the entire tunnel. Then, as quickly as it had started, it stopped.

Jay stood up. In the last few months been since he'd been coming down here, he had never heard the sobbing before—not until he found the hairpiece. He wondered if Roland might know who it belonged to or who the woman was he had heard crying. He placed the comb on one of the planks and went to close the door that led to the outside.

Leaving the two secret doors open, Jay returned to his office. He was going to go home, but the contractor would be there in less than an hour. He decided to get some paperwork done while the hour passed. He was lost in schedules when Kathy knocked on the door to announce the contractor's arrival.

"Bill, good to see you again," Jay said. "The foundation looks great on my mother's cottage."

"You, too, Jay. The framing will begin on Monday," he replied.

"I wasn't sure if you would show up today or not," Jay commented. "Everyone thinks I killed your brother."

"Not everyone. My brother made a lot of enemies over the years while serving as a selectman. Sid missed a dinner he was supposed to attend with Emmaline for her work. He should have been home with his wife and not pouring over town accounts," Bill commented. "Besides, the sheriff announced today the fingerprints on the letter opener belonged to an unknown suspect."

"I didn't do it," Jay insisted again.

"I believe you, or I wouldn't have come today," Bill stated. "Now, where is that tunnel?"

"Follow me," Jay said, heading toward the kitchen.

"Hi, Martha," Bill said as he walked by her and her full chowder pots.

She nodded her head as she kept stirring the two pots of her famous chowder.

Jay lit the lantern, and they entered the first part of the secret tunnel.

"How did you find this?" Bill marveled as he walked along.

"It was a combination of things. Actually, Ty and his uncle found it first, but they were more interested in finding the missing pirate treasure and didn't realize the whole tunnel in itself is a treasure," Jay explained as they went through the second secret door.

"Wait here," Jay instructed as he moved forward to open the door to the outside.

"This is amazing," Bill said, looking around. "And it's been hidden all these years."

"Roland Knowles did a great job recording the history of shipwrecks on the point. He really cared about the people who perished in the storms," Jay confirmed. "And now, I want people to see his historical contribution to this town a hundred years later."

"I see the lines in the dirt. Is that where you want the walls?"

"At first, I thought I could put up a four-foot wall and build the information tables on top of the wall. But the more I thought about it, I don't want things to disappear out of the tunnel. People could jump the shorter wall," Jay stated.

"Ahh, it's the times we live in that make us think that way," Bill said, shaking his head.

"I figure eight-foot-tall walls would protect the whole area, and we can build the tables in front. What do you think? Is there enough room for walls, information tables, and a walkway for people to move in and around the tunnel?" Jay asked the contractor.

"I think you need to move the protective walls two feet away from the dirt wall instead of three. The wooden tables could be built two feet wide, and you would still have plenty of room for people to walk in both directions," Bill advised.

"I need an access door built on one end to get behind the plexiglass wall for maintenance," Jay requested.

"That won't be a...problem?" Bill said, wide-eyed.

The sobbing could be heard again, and it stopped Bill mid-sentence. He looked at Jay waiting for an answer.

"I don't know what to tell you. I never heard it before today. I found a woman's hair comb buried in the dirt, and as soon as I unearthed it, the crying started," Jay stated.

"It does sound like a woman," Bill agreed. "Is she going to steal my tools like Roland did?"

"I don't know," Jay replied, laughing.

"I'm going to take some measurements and notes for what I need to purchase to complete the project. I will have an estimate drawn up for you within a couple of days," Bill said, pulling out a retractable tape measure.

The crying stopped as the two men got busy measuring the wall space. Twenty minutes later, Bill left by the door that led to the outside near the foundation of the lighthouse. Jay lit the lantern, sealed the tunnel exit behind Bill, and headed back to the café cellar.

As he closed the last door, he swore he could hear a voice pleading for help. When he paused, he didn't hear it again, so he closed the door between the cellar and the secret room and headed home to shower before his night shift began.

7

$\mathcal{J}$ay was up early Saturday morning going over the legal documents one more time before his meeting in Plymouth for the official reading of George Peterson's will. He knew this wasn't going to be a cordial meeting and was preparing himself for the worst.

For the first time since the night of the café opening, he pulled his three-piece suit out of the closet. As he passed by the window in his room, he glanced over at the reflection of his image. Staring at the suit he had on, his calm demeanor of the last few months melted away and his attorney state of mind returned.

Only for today...then it's back to café owner by the ocean, Jay told himself.

Martha was in the kitchen feeding the dogs. She smiled at her handsome son when he entered the room.

"I'll be home in a few hours," Jay told her, picking up his briefcase off the kitchen table.

"Good luck, son," Martha said. "You'll do fine."

"The will is pretty specific, but his kids could drag it out in court for years," Jay answered. "Either way, it's just one more thing to make me unpopular with the locals."

"It's not as bad as you think. The newspaper printed a retraction in this morning's edition. Don't worry about what is going on around here. Go give them heck," Martha said, cheering her son on.

"Love you, Mom," he replied, bending down kiss her cheek.

Jay turned up the radio as he drove to his appointment. The music helped him to clear his mind. Forty minutes later, he was pulling into the parking lot of the attorney's office who had drawn up George Peterson's will.

He entered the outer office and could already hear screaming coming from the inner office. The receptionist stood up and greeted him.

"Are you sure you want to go in there?" she whispered after Jay introduced himself.

"How long have they been yelling like that?" Jay inquired.

"Since they got here ten minutes ago," she answered.

"Great. Okay, let's get this over with," Jay said.

She knocked on the door, and the screaming stopped. A man in his mid-sixties opened the door. Jay entered to the glares of the Peterson siblings.

"Mr. Hallett? I'm Fred Carlson, Mr. Peterson's attorney," he said, extending his hand to Jay. "It's nice to finally meet you."

"Yes, I'm Jeremy Hallett," he confirmed.

"Great. Let's get started, can we?" Carlson asked. "Please take a seat right over there."

Jay sat facing the Petersons and their attorney. Mr. Carlson walked to the rear of his desk and sat down. He pulled out a packet of paperwork and flipped to the first page marked with a bright blue tab.

"Before we begin, Mr. Hallett, this is Greg and Amy Peterson, George's children," Carlson stated. "And Mr. White, their attorney."

"We know who he is," Amy Peterson snapped. "I wonder how my dad would feel if he knew he entrusted a killer with his estate."

"Apparently, you didn't read the paper this morning," Jay threw back at her. "I'm not a killer, and if you're not careful, you'll be involved in another lawsuit when this one is concluded."

"We're not afraid of you," Greg Peterson announced, crossing his arms in front of him. "Big shot attorney from Boston... We'll see just how good you really are."

"Greg, sit down and let Mr. Carlson speak," admonished his attorney.

"Thank you. One month before George Peterson died, I was called to his place of residence for legal counsel. While there, he was visited by Mr. Hallett and his mother, who were there to discuss an entirely different matter. Mr. Hallett, who had taken in an abandoned dog without knowing who the dog originally belonged to, had brought the dog along for the ride. During the visit, George Peterson recognized his beloved Angie, and after the dog performed a series of tricks taught to her by Mr. Peterson himself, everyone was convinced it was his dog."

"Stupid dog," Amy muttered under her breath.

"He had been promised by his children that upon his admittance to the assisted living facility, Angie would be taken care of and a loving home found for her. Neither was done. Because of the abusive treatment and abandonment of his dog, Mr. Peterson wanted his will changed."

"I can't believe this is all over a dog. Really?"

"Yes, really, Mr. Peterson. The will states you have already sold his house located at 55 Whisper Lane in Anchor Point. You took the proceeds from the sale of the house."

"We have been using the money to pay for his stay at the facility," Greg insisted. "Besides, the house had been signed over to me, so I was free to do what I wanted with it."

"The paperwork and insurance papers released to me by the facility shows that in six months, your out of pocket expenses for your father's residence there came to just under three-thousand dollars. That amount is nowhere close to the five hundred and four thousand you sold the house for."

"We kept that money in a separate savings account for future costs related to my father's upkeep," Greg stated.

"Except for the fancy car you bought yourself," his sister mumbled.

Her brother glared at her with a disgusted look.

"The will further states the remaining money from the sale of the house should be split evenly between the two of you. You will also receive fifty thousand dollars each from the bulk of the estate, which is estimated to be one point six million dollars."

"Fifty thousand dollars?" Amy screeched. "What about the rest of the money?"

"The remaining money will be entrusted to Mr. Jeremy Hallett to set up a foundation to be used at his discretion to help animal shelters take care of sick and abandoned animals."

"If you think I am going to sit back and watch all my money go to stupid animals, you are sadly mistaken," Greg threatened. "Say something, White! We hired you to fight this!"

"It's not your money. It was George's money," Jay corrected him.

"We will fight this up to the highest court," Amy added.

"There is an additional clause in Mr. Peterson's will. If you contest his decision and take the matter to court, you will automatically lose whatever money had been awarded to you in the will, and it will be added to the foundation total," Mr. Carlson stated.

"You put him up to this. You and your mother," Amy screamed, pointing her finger at Jay.

"They had nothing to do with your father's wishes. Mr. Hallett did not know until I sent him correspondence a month after your father died what had been requested of him," the attorney informed her. "Now, we need to handle this in one of two ways."

"And what way would that be?" Greg demanded, standing up.

"You can sign a release that you received your checks for the stated amount, and I will hand you a cashier's check before you leave. Or, I can rip up the checks, you can fight this in court, and lose everything, including the money for the sale of the house, which will need to be returned. Your father covered all his bases. He hand-wrote a note to Mr. Hallett stating his wishes, and he made a legally binding will with witnesses."

The two siblings looked at each other, their anger obvious to everyone around them.

"I have looked over the will, and I need to talk to my clients outside in private," Mr. White requested as he stood up.

"Fine. Mr. Hallett and I will wait for your answer," Mr. Carlson replied.

The siblings stormed out of the office, followed by their attorney. Jay could hear them arguing in the outer office. He felt bad for the receptionist who was seated at her desk and being subjected to the screaming scene unfolding in front of her.

"What do you think they will say?" Jay asked while they waited.

"If their attorney has one iota of intelligence, he will tell them to take the settlement offered to them. If they take this to court, the judge will not look too kindly on them for the reason the new will was drawn up. Truthfully, they will be getting about three-hundred thousand a piece, and I think that is being too generous, but it is not up to me," Mr. Carlson admitted.

"I agree," Jay stated.

The door opened, and the threesome filed back into the office. Amy Peterson flung herself into her chair while Greg Peterson stood behind his chair, arms crossed and glaring at Jay.

"Well?" Mr. Carlson asked.

"I have advised my clients to take the offer according to George Peterson's will. I have looked over all the corresponding legal documents and have advised them not to take this to court as I feel they will lose everything," Mr. White replied. "But it is up to them what they decide to do."

"What is your decision?" Mr. Carlson asked, turning to the Petersons.

"We have decided to accept the settlement. It will be just a matter of time until Jay Hallett is found guilty of murder and sent to jail. Then, we will proceed to recover our money," Greg stated defiantly.

"Mr. White, you have explained to your clients that once they sign the releases, they no longer have any rights to any of the money in the estate?"

"Yes, sir, I did," their attorney answered.

"You still want to sign the releases knowing the legal finality and the loss of any rights to your father's estate?" Mr. Carlson asked the siblings.

"We'll get our money eventually. You attorneys don't know every-thing," Amy muttered.

"Where is the paperwork? We'll sign… anything to get out of this stinking office," Greg snapped. "Make sure you have those checks ready to go."

"I have everything right here," Mr. Carlson insisted, opening a file folder in front of him.

Jay sat there quietly, not saying a word. He knew this fight was not over and probably never would be. Nothing was ever easy when it came to money, especially when it was over a million dollars. He had to live in the same town and knew the battle would be taken home to Anchor Point. They could make real trouble for him and his business in the future.

"Mr. White, you have looked over the releases?" Mr. Carlson asked.

"Yes, I have, and everything looks to be in order," he answered.

"Mrs. Baker, would you please step in here as a witness to the signa-tures," Mr. Carlson said to his receptionist over the phone.

She entered the office and stood to the side behind the desk.

"Gregory Peterson, please sign here on the release," Mr. Carlson requested, pointing to a specific line. "And here."

As he left the desk after signing the paperwork, Greg purposely bumped into the chair Jay was sitting in. He stared at Jay as if he were waiting for him to start something. Mr. White stepped in between the two men.

"Whose side are you on, anyway?" Greg mumbled to his attorney.

"Amy Peterson, you're next."

She signed the release and sunk back into her chair.

"Mr. White, would you please sign on the line for counsel?"

The attorney signed both releases.

"And finally, Mrs. Baker, would you sign as a witness to all the signatures?"

She signed where required and left the office. Mr. Carlson reached into the folder one more time and produced two cashiers' checks, handing one to each of the Peterson children.

"Our business is concluded. I will send copies of all the signed paperwork to your attorney, Mr. White, and he can forward everything to you," Mr. Carlson stated, standing up.

"It may be concluded in this office, but it is definitely not concluded... not by a long shot," Greg Peterson threatened as he left the office.

"Try not to spend all of our money on stupid animals before you go to jail," Amy said snidely as she followed her brother out the door.

Mr. White stood up and extended his hand to Jay and Mr. Carlson.

"Good luck, Mr. Hallett. The Peterson's are not easy people to deal with, and I don't think they understand the law as it applies to this case even though I have explained it to them several times. Mr. Carlson can get in touch with me if need be or if you have any questions," Mr. White explained. "Thank you, Mr. Carlson."

Jay and the attorney watched through the window as Mr. White was met in the parking lot by his clients and their hostility. They argued with their attorney for a good five minutes until, finally, Mr. White threw up his hands and walked away. He drove off to the screaming of the Peterson siblings.

"Now, Mr. Hallett, I have some papers that need your signatures, also."

Jay signed the papers that gave him control of the funds to be dispersed and all the other legal documents.

"I will file the legal documents and be in touch when everything is finalized. I know George trusted you explicitly to do the right thing with his estate. He loved his dog, and he knew that you loved her, too. I hope the Petersons don't give you too much trouble, although I don't believe my own words as I am saying them."

"Thank you for everything, Mr. Carlson. I look forward to hearing from you as I know the first place that will benefit from George's wishes. Our local vet in Anchor Point is struggling to stay open even though she is the only vet in the area. She has always been there for George's dog, and she will be the first to be thanked for her kindness," Jay stated.

"Have a great weekend, Mr. Hallett," Mr. Carlson said, standing and extending his hand. "Don't let a million dollars go to your head."

Jay crawled into the front seat of his car and sat there thinking about what the attorney had just said to him. He never thought about having control over someone else's money, let alone it being over a million dollars. He had to be very careful about what he did with George's money and use it to the best of his ability. If he managed the trust right, he could award the interest and maintain close to the original amount he started with so the trust could go on for many years, and many animals could be helped.

Jay started the car and drove toward home. He had promised the sheriff he would be back around noon, but that was before they found the new set of fingerprints on the letter opener. He still wanted to keep his word, knowing, in the future, his word would probably be tested by the Petersons.

8

"*How* did everything go?" Martha asked as Jay walked into the cottage.

The dogs made a beeline for their master, jumping up on him and greeting him with wet kisses. Martha pulled them off, trying to save Jay's suit from the dog hair.

"It was tense. The Petersons are not going to give up easily. They signed their releases but made the comment that when I go to jail for murder, they will go after the money again," Jay replied.

"Can they do that?"

"No, and their attorney tried to explain that to them. They basically stated that attorneys don't know everything, took their checks and stormed out."

"If you know you are in the right, I wouldn't worry about it," his mother stated.

"Where are you heading out to? Shopping for the new cottage?"

"I'm going to the beauty parlor. I haven't heard any juicy gossip for a few days and need to catch up on what's happening around town. Kathy called and had a couple of questions for you about the ticket sales for the Christmas Ball. You might want to call her back," Martha suggested.

"I'm heading over to the café now. I'll see what she needs then," Jay answered.

"Do you work tonight?"

"No, I have a dinner date with Cindy," he replied, smiling.

"It's about time you two spent some time together," Martha said, grabbing her coat and purse.

Cindy Nickerson and Jay had dated through high school. Jay broke off the relationship when he left for college and law school in Boston. When he moved back to Anchor Point, the relationship was rekindled, and they started dating again.

"Mom, you have lived here your whole life, and you know there is no time for socializing in the summer," Jay insisted.

"I know, I know, especially when it's the first year of a new business."

"But it was a great first summer," he said, hugging his mom.

"Yes, it was, and things will only get better from here on out," she agreed. "I'll see you later."

"Now, it's time to get out of this monkey suit," Jay said to the dogs, who followed him upstairs to the bedroom and jumped up on the bed.

Changing into a comfortable pair of worn jeans and a sweatshirt, he sat on the bed and rubbed each dog's belly. Deep in thought about the trust he was now in charge of, he tried to figure out how he would locate the vets or animal shelters that needed help the most.

"Let's go, girls," he said, standing up. "Let's go for a walk to the café."

The dogs heard the word 'walk' and jumped down off the bed, barking in excitement. Jay picked up Pickles, and Angie followed the two of them down the stairs. The dogs didn't need their leashes as they could walk around the back end of the café, away from the parking lot and enter in the back door of the office. The dogs could wait there while Jay took care of what he had to do.

"We have more local business today for lunch since they printed the sheriff's statement in the paper this morning," Kathy informed Jay as stood at the hostess station. "I told you it would blow over quickly."

"My mom said you had questions about the ticket sales for the ball?"

"We have sold quite a few already, but I have had several people ask if there is a discount price if they buy enough tickets to fill a whole table?"

"I never really thought about it. I guess if they buy eight tickets at once, we can give them a fifteen percent discount on the total sale. But they must buy all the tickets at the same time," Jay stated. "We already give them a break if they buy for a couple. Single tickets cost forty dollars while a couple can buy tickets for seventy dollars. Don't let them try to use both discounts. It's either one or the other."

"Yes, sir. I'll call them and let them know the answer," Kathy replied.

"How many tickets have we sold so far?" Jay inquired.

"It's the first day of the sale, and it's only September," Kathy replied. "Sales did pick up after the paper published this morning. People are so fickle."

"I'm finding that out," Jay replied, heading for the kitchen.

"The answer to your question is fifty-two," Kathy informed him as he walked away.

"Hello, Brian. Everything going okay here in the kitchen?" Jay asked, knowing Susan had requested the day off for her sister's wedding.

"Smooth and steady, sir," he answered.

"Please, call me Jay."

"Yes, sir, Jay, sir," Brian said, setting a plate of food up under the heat lamps.

Brian Stoker had applied for a job when the Shipwreck Café opened in the early summer. Before he could even report for work, he had received a call from a person claiming to be Jay's secretary telling him his services were not needed. He later questioned Jay about the situation and found out it had been a bogus phone call.

Jay offered him a year-round job when his summer job ended. With his resume being what it was, Brian was trained by Susan to be the second executive chef and in charge when she wasn't there. He had only been there for two weeks but fit right in with the rest of the staff.

"If you have any problems, call Robbie upstairs at the bar. I'm off tonight and won't be on the property," Jay informed Brian.

Brian nodded and set back to work cooking the lunch orders.

I like him… Jay heard whispered in his ear.

"Me too, Roland," Jay mumbled so that no one would hear him. "Meet me in my office."

Jay opened the door to see Roland looking out the window.

Poor Colleen...

"I have something important to ask you, my friend," Jay started. "Do you know of another ghost that resides in the cellar? A female ghost?"

No, no one else is in the building besides me...

"Are you sure? Think back over the years."

No, no one...Why?

"While I was working down in the Tunnel of Ships, I was using the heel of my shoe to make lines in the dirt for where the glass walls would be placed. I uncovered an emerald hair comb that was buried in the passageway. As soon as I found it, a woman's crying filled the tunnel. I couldn't tell where it was coming from," Jay answered.

I will search...

"Thank you, my friend. The work will begin in the tunnel on Monday, and I don't want the workers to be afraid to go down there."

Many secret passages run underneath the point, She could be anywhere.

"See what you can find out for me, please," Jay requested.

I will let you know, he said as he shimmered out.

Checking his watch, he realized he only had an hour before he was supposed to meet Cindy. He hustled the dogs out the back door and toward the cottage. As he walked, his mind returned to who could have killed Sid Swann. Right now, the only thing he was sure of was that it wasn't him. The only other suspect was Sid's wife, Emmaline.

Could she have snapped after all the constant abuse her husband had inflicted on her? The sheriff had questioned her, and she claimed to be at home alone. Was she lying? Jay had seen this before in other court cases. The wife kills the husband and then blacks out the whole event in her mind. Then again, half the town hated Sid for one reason or another, so it didn't necessarily have to be Emmaline.

They arrived at the cottage, and Jay fed the dogs an early supper. His mother wasn't home yet, so he left a note on the kitchen table telling her not to feed them again. Angie and Pickles settled down on their pillows in front of the fireplace while Jay went upstairs to take a shower and dress for his date.

He picked up Cindy, and they headed to That's Italian for supper. It was packed as it would be closing on Columbus weekend for the winter. They sat at the bar enjoying a cocktail while they waited to be called for their table.

In the back corner of the room, Jay spotted Emmaline Swann having dinner with some guy he didn't know. She wasn't hiding the fact they were together, and Jay thought that was kind of funny seeing as it was so soon after Sid's death.

"Cindy, casually look over your shoulder and tell me if you know who that is having dinner with Emmaline Swann," Jay requested.

"That's Dexter Manning, Emmaline's attorney," Cindy answered, turning back around.

"Is he from around here?"

"No, he comes from Sandwich. They had lunch at the Burger Box two days ago, and she introduced him to me," Cindy said.

"Do you think he is anything more than her attorney?" Jay asked.

"Truthfully, I have no idea," she admitted. "Why?"

"If he's a love interest, it could lead to a motive for killing her husband," Jay stated.

"Always the attorney," Cindy replied.

"Hallett. Table for two," the hostess called out.

The couple picked up their drinks and followed the hostess to their table. As Jay passed Emmaline, she smiled, picked up her cocktail and saluted Jay with it. It was almost as if she were celebrating her newfound freedom.

The couple were seated at a candlelit table and scanned over the menu. Jay settled on the veal parmigiana, and Cindy, the stuffed manicotti. Jay also ordered a bottle of merlot to go with dinner. The waitress uncorked the wine, poured them each a glass, and left them alone.

"I was going to wait until later to tell you this, but I can't," Cindy announced.

"Is something wrong?" Jay asked.

"Dad has had a stroke. You know he and my mom moved to Florida several years ago to get away from the winter's up here," Cindy started. "There is no family down there to help my mom. She's no spring chicken herself and can't do a lot of what he needs done once he comes home from rehab."

"What about a home care nurse?"

"I looked into that, but it's expensive, and the insurance my parents have will only cover twenty percent of the costs," Cindy answered.

"Your mom and dad are like second parents to me. Let me help with the cost of the nurse," Jay offered.

"My dad is a proud man and would never allow that. Which brings me to what I need to tell you," Cindy said, taking a long swig of her wine.

"You have to go to Florida and be with them," Jay surmised before Cindy could say anything.

"Yes, I do. Tom has a family here and so do my sisters. I am the only one with no family, so I am the logical person to help out," Cindy replied. "We are in the slow season, and the restaurant can get along without me for a while."

"I'm not going to say anything to make you feel bad about going," Jay said. "If it were my mom, I would do the same thing. I will miss you, though."

"I don't know exactly how long I will be down in Florida. It could be a couple of weeks to several months."

"Don't worry about things up here. Just get your dad well," Jay said, taking her hand.

"I know the holidays are approaching. If I'm not here, I want you to promise me that you will find a date for the Christmas Ball," Cindy stated firmly.

"I don't need a date to go to my own function," Jay replied. "I think you are getting way ahead of yourself."

"No, I am being realistic. I don't know how long I will be gone, and I don't want you to be tied down to someone who isn't here," Cindy explained.

"What are you saying?" Jay asked.

"I am saying I think we should be free to date other people."

"Seriously? Just like that, you made that kind of decision?" Jay inquired, caught off guard by her statement.

"It wasn't just like that. I have been thinking about it since I got the phone call from my mom," she answered. "I don't think it's fair for me to expect you to stay at home and do nothing just because I'm not here."

"I don't agree, but it's your decision if you want to break up," Jay replied. "I don't want to put any extra stress on you."

"Thank you, I appreciate that. And it's not really breaking up because we just started dating again," Cindy commented, pouring herself some more wine.

"When do you have to leave?"

"My flight is on Wednesday morning. Dad will be coming home on Thursday."

"Let's enjoy tonight, and we will worry about the future as it happens," Jay said, picking up his wine glass. "Here's to a speedy recovery for your dad."

Their glasses clinked, and before anything else could be said, their meals arrived. They made small talk the rest of the night avoiding the topic of Cindy leaving. Jay took her home right after dinner as she had lots to do before she would leave for Florida. She had to be at the Burger Box early the next morning to train one of her employees to check in orders.

In the quiet of the night, Jay gave her a kiss goodbye. She promised to call him when she landed safely in Florida. He watched her walk into her house, not knowing when he would see her again.

9

Cindy called Jay when she arrived in Florida with the bad news that her dad had had a second stroke. He would be in rehab at least six more weeks, and then it was still uncertain when he would return home.

After that one call, Jay didn't hear from Cindy again. He tried to call her, but it always went straight to messages. After five or six times trying, he accepted the fact she had meant what she said about seeing other people.

Jay had many other things to occupy his time. After a while, the last night he spent with Cindy seemed to blur into the background of the past.

He kept himself busy with the creation of the new museum, spending many hours with Roland recording the history of each item in the passage. The plexiglass walls were in place, and the tables were being constructed in front of them that would present the history of the item and what shipwreck that it came from. They were on schedule for an early spring opening.

Two different work crews had been scared off by the crying woman. Jay and Bill Swann had done a lot of the work themselves under the watchful supervision of Roland Knowles. The ghost hadn't been able to locate the sobbing spirit or communicate with her.

THE CAFÉ HAD REMAINED BUSY, mostly on the weekends. Jay picked up more shifts as a good majority of his workers had returned to school or their own countries.

He spent time out on the point checking on the construction of his mother's cottage. Bill Swann had promised it would be done before Christmas and the project was proceeding according to his schedule. It was the end of October, and the house had been framed and closed in. The electricians and plumbers were due in next.

Jay was busy doing paperwork in his office when his cell phone rang. Hoping it was Cindy, he grabbed the phone. It was Bill Swann requesting Jay come out to the site of his mother's cottage. Jay promised he'd be right there.

As he walked up to the construction site, Jay noticed a backhoe was sitting cock-eyed in what would be the driveway on the side of the house. Bill waved him over.

"What is going on?" Jay asked, pointing to the sinking machinery.

"My guys were removing the extra dirt from when the foundation was dug out, and they started to sink into the ground. We checked around and found this," Bill said, pointing to a tunnel that had been uncovered.

"It doesn't go under my mother's new place, does it?" Jay asked.

"No. It looks like the end of the tunnel stops about thirty feet from the foundation. I can't tell you too much more until we get the backhoe towed out of the hole," Bill answered.

"And when will that be?" Jay asked.

"The tow truck is on its way," Bill informed him. "Speak of the devil."

They watched as the tow truck pulled the backhoe free. It wasn't a deep hole, so it was back on level ground with just one tug. The two men walked to the edge of the cave-in. You could tell a tunnel had been there, but the end to the opening was so full of dirt, you couldn't tell how far it extended or in what direction.

"Will this affect the safety of my mother's cottage?" Jay asked the contractor.

"No, the building is on solid ground. What I can do is bring up one of my smaller tractors and dig this out for you if you have any doubts," Bill suggested.

"Truthfully, I would rather wait until spring to dig it up and see where it leads," Jay replied, thinking he would like to check his copies of the underground tunnels before he started digging everything up. "Can we move my mother's parking space to the other side of the cottage and put up some kind of decorative stone wall to prevent anyone else from driving over and into the tunnel?"

"We can do that, but the wall will cost extra," Bill answered.

"That's fine. Can you just push the extra dirt around it into the hole to seal it up for the winter?" Jay requested.

It's a dead end...

Bill looked around as he had heard the voice, as well.

"It was dug to break through a well wall when a child had fallen into it.

"Is the well near here, Roland?" Jay asked the ghost.

Somewhere... I don't remember...

"I can't believe I am standing here listening to a conversation with a ghost," Bill said, shaking his head.

"Kind of cool, isn't it?" Jay admitted.

"I knew you were around, Roland, but I have never heard you speak," Bill commented.

Must go...

The two men walked to the front of the house. Bill gave his men instructions to fill in the tunnel, but to be careful so there wouldn't be a repeat of what had just happened.

"So has the sheriff come with anything more on my brother's death?" Bill asked Jay.

"As far as I know, there are no new leads. The fingerprints they can't identify are the only thing they have to go on," Jay confirmed.

"My brother had a lot of enemies. It could be anyone. At least Emmaline doesn't have to worry about being abused anymore. I know he was my brother, but I hated the way he treated his wife. We had many fights over what he did to her," Bill admitted.

"You knew he was abusing her?" Jay asked.

"Heck, half the town knew," Bill replied. "I tried many times to get her to leave him, but she wouldn't. She was adamant about staying with him and wouldn't tell me why."

"Do you think she killed him?" Jay asked.

"No! Emmaline doesn't have a mean bone in her body," Bill declared.

"How can you be sure she didn't just snap?"

"I can't, I guess. All I know is she went to a dinner engagement, and then she was at home at its conclusion," Bill stated.

"But how do we know she was really at home and not at the town hall murdering her husband?" Jay quizzed.

Bill didn't answer right away. He shifted his weight from foot to foot for several minutes.

"You were with her, weren't you, Bill?"

"Yes, I was," he answered, eyes down.

"You know you need to tell the sheriff. You are Emmaline's alibi, and she can't be cleared if you don't admit you were with her," Jay informed him.

"I can either be her alibi or her motive," he replied. "What if they think she did it so we could be together?" he lamented.

"Were you seeing her behind Sid's back?"

"No. When I knew my brother wasn't at home, I would check on her periodically making sure she was all right," Bill admitted.

"You have to tell the sheriff everything you just told me," Jay insisted.

"You really think so? You know how the gossip flies in this town, and I don't want gossip to hurt Emmaline any more than I wanted my brother to hurt her."

"According to my mother, gossip changes hourly in this town." Jay snickered. "Gossip verses alibi? I think Emmaline would appreciate an alibi much more."

"I guess you're right. I'll go talk to the sheriff right now," Bill agreed.

Jay watched as Bill climbed up in his truck and drove away.

I don't trust him...

"I don't either, my friend. I don't know if he's just trying to give Emmaline an alibi or if he was really with her that night," Jay stated.

He knows more than he's saying...

"Time will tell, Roland, time will tell," Jay murmured.

10

It was Halloween night, and the bar at the Shipwreck Café was hopping. The first annual costume party was in full swing, and over one hundred people had shown up in costume to celebrate. They had closed off the entire second floor for the function.

The costumes ranged from totally gross zombies to a humorous pile of leaves that left a trail of dead leaves everywhere the person walked. Robbie and two other bartenders were dressed as pirates and were at full throttle serving drinks to the costumed patrons. Their tip jars were overflowing and had already been emptied twice.

Jay was dressed as Zorro, who had been one of his childhood favorites. His black cape swished as he moved about the room socializing with all his customers. His black hair was perfect for his chosen costume, but the little black mask couldn't hide his bright blue eyes. He danced with many women during the night but still couldn't rid his mind of Cindy.

At midnight, Jay handed out the prizes for the various categories of costumes and the bar closed at one. By one-thirty, the band had left, and the staff was cleaning up and resetting the dining room for tomorrow's lunch crowd. Robbie waved Jay over to the end of the bar.

"Weren't you the popular dancing partner tonight?" Robbie kidded his brother.

"I'm beat. This socializing is hard work," Jay admitted.

"Did you happen to notice the person in the mummy costume tonight?" Robbie asked, refilling the beer cooler.

"There were like four mummies here tonight. Which one?"

"The shorter mummy who was cozied up to the pharaoh with the thick makeup all night," Robbie stated.

"I saw them on the dance floor. Why?"

"Do you know who the mummy was?" Robbie asked.

"The person was covered from head to toe in gauze. I didn't get close enough to see who it was under the disguise."

"It was Emmaline Swann. I served her and her friend quite a few drinks in the corner throughout the night. I overheard her calling him 'my love' on one of my trips to the table."

"Isn't that interesting?" Jay mumbled. "I wonder if it was her attorney I saw her with at the restaurant. I wish I had paid more attention to what was happening around me. Did you recognize the guy?"

"No, I didn't. Lighten up, big brother. This is the first time I have seen you enjoy yourself and let loose in a long while. I just figured you would want to know what I saw and heard."

"I'm going to see the sheriff tomorrow, and I'll tell him what you told me," Jay stated.

"So how many phone numbers did you collect tonight?" Robbie asked, pulling slips of paper out of his pocket. "I saw some fine looking women handing them to you."

"I don't know. Five or six, I guess." Jay sighed. "Not that I really care."

"Come on, man. She told you to move on, and that's what you need to do. Cindy hasn't returned any of your calls, and it's been almost two months since she went to Florida. She set the rules before she left, and you need to let her go," Robbie advised his older brother.

"I know. It's just hard. I thought when I came back here, we would pick up where we left off. She seemed happy we were starting to date again and then, boom. The only thing I can think of is she knows she is not coming back and couldn't tell me," Jay stated.

"She cut you loose, and you need to accept that...just saying," Robbie replied.

"We're heading home," yelled one of the waitresses. "See you tomorrow for lunch."

Strange people...

Jay and Robbie turned to see Roland standing at the end of the bar.

"It was a costume party, Roland. Just people dressing up and having a good time," Robbie explained.

Strange people... he repeated as he shimmered out.

"I'm going to cash out the registers and head home," Jay said.

"I'll be in bed and snoring before you leave the building," Robbie laughed. "See you tomorrow."

The two registers were full. It had been one of the busiest days since Labor Day Weekend, and tomorrow's deposit was going to be a healthy one. Jay smiled as he zippered the bank bag closed. Things were getting back to normal for both him and his business.

He shut the lights off on the second floor and headed to his office to lock the day's receipts in the safe. After a trip to the sheriff's office and the bank in the morning, Jay would return to the café and begin preparing for the upcoming holiday season. The Seashell Giving Tree had to be assembled in the waiting area and promotions for the Seashell Christmas Ball had to be confirmed. Things were looking up. If only Cindy were here to share it with.

The next morning, Jay dropped the deposit off at the bank and drove to the sheriff's office. The station was locked up tight, and no one was around, not even dispatch. He walked across the street to the Coffee Café to see if anyone knew where Sheriff Boyd and his deputies were.

The place was abuzz about something. Jay walked up to the register to find out what was going on in town.

"Jay, over here."

Tom Nickerson, Cindy's brother and one of Boyd's deputies, was waving Jay over to where he was eating his breakfast. Jay slid into the booth and looked to Tom for answers.

"Nancy, bring Jay a cup of coffee, please," Tom requested of one of the waitresses that passed by where they were seated.

"What is going on, Tom? Gossip central is alive and doing well this morning." Jay chuckled.

"The office was called at six-thirty this morning to go to the Swann house. Emmaline is dead. She was strangled sometime between three and six this morning," Tom answered, solemnly.

"That doesn't leave very much time as she and her date didn't leave the café until almost one o'clock in the morning," Jay suggested.

"You saw her last night?"

"I didn't, but Robbie did. They were at the costume party, and he served them drinks all night," Jay replied.

"Did Emmaline and this date leave together?" Tom asked.

"I don't know. You'd have to ask Robbie," Jay stated. "I went to the station to tell Stephen what Robbie saw and heard last night, but no one was there."

"Saw and heard?"

"Yes, he saw Emmaline and this guy acting cozy all night, and he heard her call him 'my love,'" Jay answered. "Is the sheriff still at the Swann residence?"

"Yea, they are processing the scene," Tom answered in between bites of his toast. "I wouldn't go over there. You were a suspect in Sid's death, and now his wife is dead. If I were you, I would stay as far away as possible from that place right now."

"I have no intention of going over there. Just do me a favor and tell Stephen what I said, okay?"

"I will. I'm heading back there after I eat. I had the night shift, and this is the first break I have had since six last night," Tom said. "The sheriff will probably pay Robbie a visit sometime today to ask him some questions."

"I'll let Robbie know," Jay said, standing up. "Thanks for the coffee."

Robbie was restocking the bar that had been all but emptied at last night's costume party. Jay told him what happened to Emmaline and gave him the message the sheriff would be around to see him. Next, he went to the kitchen to see if his mom was there. Martha was stirring two large kettles of her famous homemade chowder, waiting for them to thicken to the right consistency.

"I have to keep my arm muscles even," she joked, holding up a dripping spoon in each hand.

"Mom, have you been here since seven?" Jay asked.

"Yes, is something wrong? Are the dogs okay?" she asked.

"Emmaline Swann was murdered last night in her home. She was strangled," Jay replied.

"Oh, I am so sorry. That poor woman had enough grief in her life being married to Sid. And now, when she is finally free, this happens. What a pity," she said. "Do they know who did it?"

"No, not as far as I know anyway," Jay said, stealing some chowder from the closest pot to him.

"I don't understand this place anymore. It used to be such a safe place to live. There have been no murders in Anchor Point since I was a young girl and then two this past summer and now two more," Martha complained. "I am really beginning to wonder if I should have moved to Florida even without Theresa."

I'll protect you, Martha...

"Thank you, Roland. I appreciate it," Martha said, smiling. "I feel safer already."

He had a tattoo... on his forearm.

"Who does? What are you talking about?" she asked.

The man in the corner...

"Are you talking about the man at the costume party last night? The man who was with Emmaline?" Jay asked.

I heard you talking to Robbie... ask him if he saw the tattoo.

"What did it look like, Roland?"

Don't know... Wasn't close enough.

"Mom, I need to go talk to Robbie," Jay stated.

"As soon as I am finished here, I am going to the beauty parlor. I'll see what I can find out and let you know," Martha commented.

"Thanks, Mom."

Jay returned to the bar looking for his brother.

"Robbie, are you here?" Jay yelled.

He popped up from behind the bar with a wrench in his hand.

"Don't yell like that. I almost whacked my head on the bottom of the sink," he replied.

"Something wrong with the sink?" Jay asked, looking at the wrench.

"Just a small leak. I can take care of it. What did you want?"

"When you served Emmaline and her guest drinks, did you notice a tattoo on his forearm?" Jay inquired.

"Yea, he had one, but I couldn't tell you exactly what it was. Most of it was hidden under his costume sleeve. I think it was tools or something like that," Robbie answered.

"Tools?"

Yea, like hammers and screwdrivers. You know, tools," Robbie confirmed.

"Thanks. Are you sure you don't need me to call the plumber?" Jay asked, not wanting a flooded café.

"I got this, dude," Robbie insisted, disappearing behind the bar again.

Jay smiled. His brother hadn't called him dude since the argument they had on the beach. Back then, Jay had been so high strung that it bothered him when Robbie wouldn't use his real name. This time, he didn't mind it. He felt closer to his brother than he had over the last twenty years, and if Robbie wanted to call him dude, it was okay.

"Anyone around?" yelled a voice from the first floor.

"Stephen, we're up here at the bar. Come on up," Jay yelled back.

Sheriff Boyd walked over to the brothers. He looked tired and frazzled. He plopped down on a bar stool and sighed.

"Are you okay?" Robbie asked him.

"Just tired, I guess. The case trying to find Sid's murderer is going nowhere and now Emmaline is dead. I don't know how much more this town can take," he replied. "I don't know how much more I can take."

"Did anything at the scene help you?" Jay asked, sitting next to his friend.

"Nothing. She was strangled in bed. The coroner places the time of death between three and six this morning," the sheriff started. "We have some DNA that we took off the sheets and have sent out for testing, but other than that, nothing."

"Have you eaten anything today?" Jay asked.

"No, I have been at the Swann house all morning," the sheriff answered.

"While you talk to Robbie about the guy who was here with Emmaline, I'll get you some of my mom's chowder. She just finished a new batch. I'll be right back," Jay suggested.

Jay returned and set a bowl of chowder and a fresh tossed salad in front of the sheriff. Robbie added a soda to the mix. While the sheriff ate, they continued to discuss the case.

"Whoever did this was not in a good frame of mind," he said between bites.

"How so?" Jay asked.

"The coroner said that Emmaline was strangled with so much force that it crushed her windpipe. The murderer was enraged," the sheriff replied. "She knew her killer. There was no sign of forced entry."

"I wonder if she took the guy home that she was here drinking with all night," Robbie speculated.

"Could be. But it seems you were the only one close enough to him to tell us anything."

Tell him about the tattoo...

"Hello, Roland. It's nice to see you again. Well, you know what I mean. What tattoo?" the sheriff asked.

The man in the corner had a tattoo...

"What's he talking about?" Boyd asked.

"Emmaline and her male friend sat in that corner all night at the costume party," Robbie said, pointing to a spot to the right of the bar. "I served them drinks, but the dude had on so much face makeup I couldn't tell you who he was."

"Face makeup?"

"Yea, he was dressed up as a pharaoh. He had on bronze makeup, thick black eye-liner, and a wig held in place by a snake headband," Robbie explained.

"What about this tattoo?" Boyd asked, scraping the bottom of his chowder bowl clean.

"Like I told Jay, I didn't get a good look at it because the sleeve of his costume covered it most of the time. From what I could see, it looked like tools," Robbie answered.

"Roland, could you see the tattoo?" Boyd asked the ghost.

No... just could see it was there.

The sheriff slugged down what was left of the soda and stood up.

"Thank you for lunch. I hadn't realized how hungry I was," Boyd stated. "Robbie, if you think of anything else, give me a call."

"Will do," he answered, clearing the dishes off the bar.

"Jay, I'll be in touch. Have a good day, Roland," Boyd said as he disappeared down the stairs.

"I'm going to check on the kitchen, and then I'm out of here for the day," Jay said to Robbie. "I'll see you sometime tomorrow."

"Hot plans for the night off?" Robbie teased.

"Yea, I'm going to drink a few beers with two dogs and look over the maps of the underground tunnels," Jay answered. "I want to find where the well is located behind mom's cottage."

I can show you...

"Roland, I forgot you were here with us. Do you remember where it is, my friend?"

I remember...

"Can you show me where it is when the construction crew is gone?" Jay requested.

It's dried up and filled in... has been since the little boy fell in.

"Do you remember what year it was?"

1909...right before I died.

"Great. I will meet you out on the point this afternoon," he confirmed.

Jay let the dogs out when he returned home. He sat on his back deck, chilly as it was, and watched them playing with Colleen, the girl ghost. It had taken a while, but she wasn't afraid to appear in front of Jay anymore. He knew she must have figured out that he wouldn't bother her, and her love of visiting the dogs outweighed her fear of the living.

"Jay, are you here?" Martha yelled from the kitchen.

"Out here on the deck. I'll be right in," he answered. "Angie! Pickles! It's time to go inside, come on."

"What's up, Mom?"

"Wait until you hear what I learned at the beauty parlor today," she said, unpacking the groceries that she had brought home with her.

"You mean at Gossip Central?" He chuckled.

"Call it what you want, but women tend to run their mouths when getting their hair done," she said with a laugh. "I guess it's because there are no men around, and they feel safe to say what they think."

"So, what did you find out?" Jay asked, picking up one of the apples his mom had just taken out of the paper bag.

"Emmaline Swann had been involved in an affair for over a year," Martha replied.

"Do they know with who?"

"That's the funny part. This man was seen sneaking out of Emmaline's house in the middle of the night many times, but it was always too dark for anyone to see who he was," she replied. "He always left the house on foot and never drove a car so that no one could see a plate number."

"Do you think Sid knew?"

"I'm sure he did. That's probably why he beat her all the time," Martha replied. "Not to change the subject, but have you heard from Cindy?"

"No, not a word," Jay sighed.

"I have."

"Mom, you heard from her and didn't tell me? What did she say? Why hasn't she returned any of my calls?" Jay asked.

"I just talked to her this morning. Her dad had another series of small strokes and is not in particularly good shape. They don't know how much longer he will be with us," Martha answered.

"Does that mean she will bring her mother back here?"

"No, her mother made it quite clear that she will not move back to Anchor Point. Cindy has agreed to stay with her mom until, well, you know, the end," Martha stated. "She has taken a job down there and will not be back. She wanted me to tell you that she has moved on, and she wants you to do the same thing. She requested that you stop calling her."

Jay put the apple down on the table. He didn't say anything, but his mom could tell he was hurting inside.

"I'm so sorry, Jay, but she wanted me to be the one to tell you," Martha said, hugging her son.

"I kind of knew something was going on when she didn't return my phone calls. I guess it really is over, and I have to move on," Jay sighed.

Susan really likes you, you know...

"Hello, Roland," Martha said. "Yes, I noticed that, too."

Hello, Martha. Nice to see you.

"Seriously you two? I can't even get over one break-up, and you two are trying to set me up with someone else?" Jay moaned.

Just saying...

"I like Susan. She's a nice girl," Martha said to Roland.

She is very nice and a hard worker...

"Okay, you two can continue this conversation without me. I'll be in the living room looking at maps," Jay said, grabbing a beer out of the fridge and treats for the dogs.

The dogs followed Jay and jumped up on the couch waiting for their treats. He opened the safe and took out the copies of the journal pages he had made before he turned the book over to the sheriff to be used as evidence in Bea Thomas's murder.

He sat on the couch with a dog on either side of him. They happily gnawed on their treats as Jay perused the pages that showed the underground tunnels around his property. Two hours passed as he poured over the diagrams.

"Roland said to meet him out near my cottage before it gets dark," Martha said on her way to her bedroom. "He said you would know why."

"Thanks. I lost track of time," he said, standing up. "Come on, girls. I'll take you out before I go."

Jay arrived at the construction site twenty minutes later. He walked around to the side yard where the tunnel had been discovered. Bill had stretched a temporary orange mess fence around the area. He walked along the outline of the cave-in until he couldn't tell where the tunnel was anymore.

It doesn't go too much further...

"The boy didn't survive, did he?" Jay asked.

No, he didn't. They dug the tunnel to drain the well to recover the body.

"And the well was never used again?"

No...

"I was looking at your journal and the way the tunnels run under the point. The way I figure it is the well would have been a perfect place to hide the treasure," Jay suggested.

That would have been too easy...

"Where is the well located? It doesn't show on any of the maps in your journal," Jay inquired. "It's almost like you wanted to keep it hidden for some reason."

No reason... Just bad memories for everyone that lived in town... better forgotten.

"Are we close to it? I would like to mark where it is," Jay said, walking forward.

Do you promise not to dig up the well again?

"I can't promise that, Roland. There might be some historical finds buried down there," Jay commented. "Not to mention the missing treasure."

The treasure is not there. Why do you not believe me?"

"Because you said that no one would ever find the treasure again. You would see to it. So, even if I'm right, you won't tell me."

The well is ten feet in front of you. There is no treasure, only a place of death for a small child. I cannot be here if you dig it up again.

Jay watched Roland shimmer out. He could tell the ghost was upset with him. Maybe the well was just that—a place of death. Jay would have to find that out for himself. Not today, but sometime soon.

Jay collected two good-sized rocks and placed them where he believed the well was. He knew what the placement of the rocks meant, but it wouldn't be obvious to anyone else looking at the area. It just looked like two rocks that randomly landed on the ground.

As he stood there near the markers, he thought he could hear a faint crying. It didn't sound like a small child's cry, but a woman's cry. It sounded like the crying from the tunnel only muffled.

There must be another tunnel in the area that leads to the ones under the café, Jay thought.

Jay returned to his cottage with the intention of studying the maps the rest of the night and trying to connect the tunnels on his property.

At the café, Susan was down in the cellar, checking the stock on hand and assembling an order to be placed in the morning. She was moving the can goods around, counting what was on the shelves when the structure gave way and toppled on top of her. She was knocked out cold.

Roland had been watching her from behind the wine locker. When the shelving collapsed, and Susan didn't move, he knew what he had to do.

11

Roland shimmered in next to Jay, blowing all the papers he had laid out on the coffee table onto the floor.

"Roland! I know you're mad at me, but this? Really?" Jay exclaimed.

Susan... hurt.

"What do you mean? Where is she?" Jay asked, throwing the papers he was holding on the couch.

She's in the cellar... not moving... hurry.

Jay yelled to his mother to call 911 and send them to the café. He ran out the door, barefoot and with no coat on. It was November, and he didn't stop to think how cold it would be outside. He just kept running.

Tearing through the front door, he ran past everyone in the kitchen and descended the cellar stairs yelling Susan's name as he went. Brian followed close behind to see if he could help in any way.

Roland was floating next to where Susan was laying. Brian stopped short in his tracks when he saw the ghost. He had only been there a short time and had heard the stories but had never actually seen him.

"Brian, snap out of it and help me lift this off Susan," Jay ordered.

The two men struggled to pick up the heavy metal unit and move it off their fallen co-worker. They pushed the cans aside and cleared the way for the paramedics. Susan still hadn't stirred.

"They are down in the cellar," Martha said from the top of the stairs. "Jay, the paramedics are here."

Susan came to as she was being hooked up to the machines that would check her vitals. The first face she saw was Jay's, and she could see how worried he was. She could also see that he had no shoes on and started to laugh, clutching her rib area as she did.

"What is so funny?" Jay asked.

"Where are your shoes?" she asked.

"I guess I forgot them," Jay admitted, smiling. "Roland said that you had been hurt, and I guess I didn't think about shoes. I just wanted to get over here."

"Roland said?" Brian echoed. "You talk to him?"

"Her vitals are stable, but I think she has some broken ribs. That's a huge welt on her forehead so she may have a concussion. She needs to have x-rays done and may have to stay overnight at the hospital for observation," the technician announced.

"But work. I'm on twelve-hour shifts for the next three days," Susan moaned.

"I'll cover your shifts," Brian said, still looking around the cellar for Roland, who had disappeared when the paramedics arrived.

"Don't you worry about work. I'll follow you to the hospital to see what the doctors say," Jay commented.

"I hope you are going to go home and get some shoes first," Susan said, smiling at her boss.

The paramedics strapped her to a gurney, and then they hoisted her up the stairs and out to the ambulance. Jay stood at the back of the ambulance, and as the vehicle doors were closing, he assured Susan he would see her shortly.

His mom walked up from behind and put her arms around him as they watched the ambulance pull away. He felt the cold for the first time since he left the house and shivered.

"Let's get you home," his mom suggested, gently pushing her son toward his cottage. "She'll be okay thanks to Roland."

"I was scared when I saw her lying there motionless," Jay admitted as they walked.

"Maybe, deep down, you do have feelings for Susan and just never admitted it to yourself because of Cindy. You do have a lot in common you know," Martha stated.

"No, I don't know. I don't know that much about her except what a great executive chef she is and how well she is liked by everyone," Jay admitted.

"Have you noticed lately that she has been coming into the office even when the dogs are in there?" Martha asked.

"Come to think of it, yes. But she is allergic to dogs. At least, that's she told me," Jay answered, opening the cottage door for his mom.

"She loves Angie and Pickles. She also wanted to be able to spend more time with you, so she went to the doctor and is taking pills to help with the allergy. Don't you dare tell her I told you or she'll never trust me again," Martha insisted.

"Why hadn't I noticed these things?" Jay asked as the dogs welcomed them home.

"You were so busy feeling sorry for yourself over the things you couldn't have that you didn't notice what was right in front of your face," Martha lectured.

"I guess you're right... as usual." Jay smiled. "I'm going to get dressed and head to the hospital. I'm not sure when I will be home."

"Tell Susan I am thinking of her," Martha said, calling the dogs to follow her to her bedroom.

"I will."

Jay arrived at the hospital only to have to sit in the waiting area as Susan was still being examined, and they were waiting for the x-rays to be read. He fidgeted in his chair, his mind floating back to when his mom was attacked during the summer, and they didn't know if she would survive or not. He hated hospitals.

Grabbing a cup of coffee out of the vending machine, he read various magazines for the next hour waiting to hear something on his employee.

"Mr. Hallett," the receptionist called out from behind her desk.

"I'm Jay Hallett," he said, standing up.

"Susan Myers is requesting to see you. She is in the yellow unit, cubicle fourteen. Go through those doors, turn right and then straight ahead to the yellow unit," she advised.

"Thank you," Jay replied as he opened the doors.

He found Susan's cubicle with no problem. She smiled when she spotted him peeking in between the curtain and the wall.

"Can I come in?" he asked.

"Please do. There is nothing on television this time of night except news. I'm so bored," she answered.

"Have you heard anything from the doctors yet?"

"Not yet. Hopefully soon." She sighed.

"I am so sorry about what happened. I thought I had bolted the shelving to the wall securely. I even used extra-long bolts," Jay explained.

"Things happen. I guess maybe I shouldn't have stood on the unit's bottom shelf to get to the cans on the top shelf," she admitted. "Maybe we can extend the shelves to be longer instead of taller like they were."

"Sounds like a plan," Jay agreed.

"Knock, knock. Can I come in?" the doctor asked.

"Only if you have good news," Susan answered with a smile.

"Good news, bad news—a little of both," he said, flipping the papers on his clipboard.

"What's the bad news?" she asked.

"You have two broken ribs and one fractured rib. You are a very lucky woman that none of them punctured a lung in the fall."

"What's the good news?"

"The rest of your injuries are not life-threatening in any way, but we do want you to stay here tonight so we can keep an eye on you. You are going to be one sore woman over the next few days," he replied.

"When can I return to work?" Susan inquired.

"Not for a couple of weeks, I'm afraid, maybe longer. You have to give those ribs a chance to heal before you move around too much."

"Can't you just wrap them or something to keep them in place?"

"We don't wrap broken ribs anymore. It can lead to pneumonia because the bandages don't allow for your lungs to fill to full capacity," the doctor informed her.

"Don't worry. Susan will stay at home until she gets the all clear to come back to work. I will see to it," Jay announced. "With full pay."

"I'm going to arrange for a room for the night. I'll be back," the doctor said.

"With pay? Nice touch, boss." Susan smiled.

"I meant it. Don't you dare set foot back in that kitchen until you are fully recovered," Jay replied. "If it takes weeks or a couple of months, you will receive workman's comp while you are out."

"I have to admit, it does hurt just to breathe," Susan replied.

"I'm sure they will give you something for the pain when you get settled into your room," Jay said. "I'll call you tomorrow, and if they release you, I'll pick you up and take you home."

"I can take a taxi," she stated. "Uh, no I can't. My purse and phone are at the café."

"See, it's just meant to be that I come get you. You still know my cell number?"

"Yes, and I'll call you when I know anything."

"Good."

"Jay, before you go, I need to tell you something."

"It can wait until tomorrow," he insisted.

"No, it can't. There's talk around the kitchen that Emmaline was killed by her secret lover. I know who that secret lover is," she claimed.

"You know who she was seeing? How?" Jay asked.

"Last spring, I catered a luncheon at the Swann house for the Anchor Point Garden Club. I was out on the veranda setting the tables when I heard a man and woman arguing in the pool house. I knew it wasn't Sid because he had left for work after complaining that he wasn't going to be caught dead around so many cackling women."

"Did you see who it was?"

"Yes, I did. I don't think they knew anyone was in earshot and they were arguing about Emmaline leaving Sid. She refused, and he stormed out of the pool house. He was in the middle of threatening her when he spotted me standing there."

"Who was it?"

"Ross Morris. He works for the town. He's the one you see sitting at the gatehouse collecting fees at the town dump."

"I don't know him," Jay replied. "Do you think they were still seeing each other?"

"I saw them talking after Sid's funeral."

"You don't know if he has a tattoo, do you?" Jay asked.

"That I don't know," she said, closing her eyes, the medicine starting to take effect.

"Get some rest. I'll talk to you tomorrow," Jay said, patting her hand. "By the way, Mom says she's thinking of you."

"I love your mom," she mumbled, drifting off to sleep.

Jay drove home thinking about what Susan had just told him. He called the sheriff and passed on the information that he had just received. The sheriff knew who Ross Morris was and said he would talk to him in the morning.

Jay entered the cottage quietly so as not to disturb the dogs and wake his mother. He climbed into bed and looked around the room. It was lonely on the bed without Angie and Pickles.

Is Susan okay?

Roland was standing at the footboard.

"She has some broken ribs and was pretty banged up. Susan will be out of work for quite a while," Jay replied. "Thank you for coming to get me tonight, Roland."

Such a nice girl... I had to help her.

"She's staying in the hospital tonight," Jay stated. "I'll let you know when I hear anything new."

Good night...

Jay laid down for some much-needed sleep.

12

The next morning, Jay met his mother at the café to begin decorating for Christmas. The Seashell Giving Tree was going to be the first decoration to go up. The scallop shells had been numbered on the inside of the shell, and the corresponding list was on Jay's desk in the office. The fake tree stood twelve feet tall and was placed just to the left of the hostess station.

Red and green lights along with gold garland were wound around the tree from top to bottom. The scallop shells, each representing an individual child or family, were the only ornaments to be placed on the tree. As a shell was claimed by a secret Santa, an angel would be put in its place. Jay hoped by the time Christmas Eve arrived, the tree would be covered with all angels and no shells.

A shiny gold tree skirt had been placed around the base. Kathy had been busy wrapping empty boxes to put under the tree. They all stepped back to admire the finished product.

"It's beautiful," Martha stated.

"Let's just hope those empty boxes will be replaced by full boxes with secret Santa donations by Christmas Eve," Jay replied.

Sheriff Boyd walked through the front door and whistled when he saw the tree.

"That's a beauty," he complimented. "Let me be the first one to take a shell off the tree."

He read the back of the shells and picked one with a young boy, age five listed on it. He handed the shell to Kathy, who went to the office to get the corresponding list.

"I have two sons. I don't know anything about what girls would like for Christmas. Five-year-old boys I can shop for. Not that I do the shopping, mind you. My wife does that." He chuckled.

"Maybe your wife would like to shop for a little girl for a change," Martha suggested.

"You're right," he agreed, walking back to the tree to take a second shell.

"Stephen, you don't need to take more than one," Martha said. "I was just suggesting that your wife might like something different.

"It's okay, Martha. I have had a blessed year and can do this," he said, handing the second shell to Kathy who had returned with the list.

"Is there a reason you stopped by?" Jay asked.

"I wanted to check on Susan, and I had an interesting morning at the dump," he replied.

"I haven't heard from the hospital yet," Jay informed him.

"I went to the dump to talk to Ross. Yesterday was his day off, and he didn't show up for work today," the sheriff started. "His boss called his home phone and his cell phone, but he didn't answer either call."

"Do you think he's taken off because he killed Emmaline?" Martha inquired.

"I don't know, but it does look suspicious on his part. I have put out an APB on him," Boyd stated. "And, he did have a tattoo. Co-workers told me that he had crossed hammers on his right forearm. He used to work in construction before he landed the town job."

"It must have been him here with Emmaline the night of the costume party," Jay surmised.

"We'll find him," the sheriff said. "Got to run."

He left with his two shells in hand. Jay turned to his mom and handed her two angels to put on the tree. Martha put them in the empty spots where the scallop shells once were.

"Three down, ninety-seven to go," she announced.

"Two down, Mom, not three," Jay corrected her.

She reached up and took one of the shells that had a family of four listed on it.

"You forgot. I sold my house this year, and I want to pay it forward. I know the new cottage being built has to be paid for, but there is plenty left over to help someone else have a good Christmas."

"Mom, you are awesome," Jay said, hugging her and kissing the top of her head.

"It's almost time to open for lunch. We will continue our decorating tomorrow morning," she replied, brushing off the compliment and heading for the kitchen.

Kathy tucked the shell list under the drawer of the register so she would have easy access to it if a customer came in at lunch and wanted to take a shell. Jay placed a third angel on the tree and tucked the box with the rest of the angels under the hostess station.

"I'll be in the kitchen trying to help Brian as best as I can. I guess I am going to have to learn as I go." Jay chuckled.

"I don't think they will need you," Kathy informed him. "Mandy, the lead sous chef, has stepped up to help Brian get the kitchen through until Susan comes back."

"I guess they don't want me in the kitchen," Jay joked.

"Maybe so," Kathy agreed.

"I'll be in my office paying bills," Jay said. "Call me if you need anything."

Jay was able to catch up on all the current week's paperwork and start on the following week's work. He sorted three days' worth of mail and came across an envelope from George Peterson's attorney, Mr. Carlson.

The manila envelope contained copies of all the filed legal documents as well as the bank information giving him full control over the trust fund. He sat back in his chair looking at the bank statement and the accompanying blank checks.

Check number one would be delivered this afternoon to Doctor Carsen in Anchor Point. The Sandwich Animal Hospital had taken away much of her business as they had bigger and better equipment at their disposal. Maybe this money would bring her office equipment up to date and keep her hospital open to take care of the local animals. She loved her patients. You could see it in her eyes as she looked at them and hear it in her voice as she talked to them.

Feeling good about his first decision, he wrote out a thirty-thousand-dollar check to the Anchor Point Animal Hospital. After all, Angie and Pickles needed her here and so did the rest of the local community who loved their pets.

Before he left for the vet's office, he called the hospital to check on Susan. The call was transferred to her room, and she answered the phone on the second ring. She informed her boss they were going to keep her another twenty-four to forty-eight hours as one of the broken ribs was closer to her lung than they first thought. She asked about the café, and Jay assured her the kitchen was being well taken care of in her absence and told her not to worry.

"Geez, will I still have a job when I can come back?" She sighed.

"Only if you promise not to file a lawsuit against me or the café." Jay chuckled.

"Not happening, boss. It was an accident and nothing more."

"I was only joking about the lawsuit. Your job is secure. Just take it easy, and I will call you in the morning," Jay replied.

Jay checked the kitchen, and Brian insisted that everything was going smoothly. He told his mom where he was heading and that he'd be back later. Martha told him she was almost done making the chowder and that she would go home and take the dogs out so he didn't have to.

"Kathy, if you need me, call my cell. I'll be back in an hour or so," Jay said, holding the front door open for customers entering for lunch.

The animal hospital was almost devoid of customers. One woman sat in the corner reassuring her cat who was meowing loudly from his carrier. Another older gentleman sat on the other side of the room with a metal cage balancing on his lap. A fat white rat was scurrying around in the straw at the bottom of the cage.

"Mr. Hallett, nice to see you again," the receptionist said as he approached the counter. "What? No Angie or Pickles with you?"

"Not today. I am here to see Dr. Carsen. Is she available for a few minutes?" Jay asked.

"Let me check. She's with a patient right now, but she should have five minutes free when she's done."

"That's all I need, thank you," Jay stated.

"Have a seat, and I'll call you when she's ready to see you."

Jay walked over to the man with the cage. He thought he looked familiar and introduced himself.

"I know who you are, Mr. Hallett, but apparently, you don't recognize me," he said.

"You look familiar, but I can't place a name," Jay replied.

"Does Mr. Edwards ring a bell?"

"You worked at the penny candy store with George Peterson," Jay exclaimed.

"Yes, I did. And you were one of our best customers when you were younger."

"I knew you looked familiar." Jay smiled. "And who is this?'

"This is Pickett. He's an albino rat. I think he has cancer. I want Dr. Carsen to look at him. I don't know how much she can do with no x-ray machine on the premises. I almost took Pickett to Sandwich, but I love Dr. Carsen and don't want to desert her like others have."

"She has no x-ray machine?" Jay asked.

"No, she doesn't. It broke down, and she hasn't been able to fix it."

"Well, she will have one shortly, Mr. Edwards. You don't have to worry about Dr. Carsen anymore," Jay said, patting his shoulder. "Thank you for your help."

"You're welcome. I don't know what I did, but you're welcome," he said, smiling.

"Mr. Hallett, the doctor will see you now."

"Jay, please," he said as he followed the receptionist to the Dr.'s office.

"Have a seat, and she'll be right in."

Dr. Carsen entered the office and smiled when she saw Jay.

"How are Angie and Pickles?" she asked, sitting in the chair opposite Jay.

"They are doing fine. Spoiled more than ever by my mother," he answered, chuckling.

"So, what can I do for you today?"

"Mr. Edwards tells me that your x-ray machine is down, and you haven't had the money to fix it," Jay started.

"Yes, it died about three months ago. It was a second-hand machine, but I thought that it would last longer than it did." She sighed.

Jay reached into his pocket and brought out the check.

"This is the reason I am here," he admitted, handing her the check.

Her eyes grew wide as she looked at the written amount.

"What is this?" she stuttered.

"This is a gift from George Peterson. He appreciated the way you took care of his dog when he was alive. He wanted you to be able to continue taking care of the animals in Anchor Point," Jay explained.

"I can't believe this. Mr. Peterson told me he would take care of this animal hospital, but then his kids sent him away. I never expected anything like this," she said, tearing up.

"When I wrote the amount, I didn't know that your x-ray machine was down. Purchasing a new one would take a big chunk out of the check you are holding. I want you to order a new machine and have the bill sent to me. I will pay for it out of the trust that George set up for the animals. I want you to use that check for supplies or to update equipment that you need to bring your customers back from Sandwich," Jay advised.

"I can't believe this," she repeated. "A new x-ray machine, too?"

"There is one catch. You can never tell anyone about the donation or where it came from. It has to remain a secret," Jay admonished.

"I won't breathe a word. Now I can take care of my patients the way they deserve." She smiled. "Thank you, Mr. Hallett. Thank you."

"It wasn't my doing, it was George's. Say a little prayer of thanks to him later," Jay replied. "Order that machine and let me know when you need the payment."

He stood up to leave.

"You have a real loyal customer in Mr. Edwards out there. He is afraid his rat has cancer, and he knew you might not be able to diagnose him properly without an x-ray machine, but he came here anyway. Make sure you assure him you will be able to take care of Pickett properly in the very near future," Jay advised. "He's a good person."

"I will, and thank you again," she said, shaking his hand.

He waved to Mr. Edwards on the way out. Jay felt good inside. He hoped he would always feel this way when he handed out the trust money and that it didn't get old. George Peterson had given him a rare opportunity in life. The chance to help animals that can't help themselves. This was one job Jay would gladly carry out throughout his entire life.

13

It was Sunday morning, and Jay had host duty at the front door for lunch. Kathy went to church on Sunday mornings and would be in for the evening shift at four. Jay and his mom had finished decorating the first floor for Christmas.

The banisters going to the second floor were draped in pine boughs and holly. Every four feet, a large red velvet bow had been attached to the pine. Silk red poinsettias were placed on every other stair, even numbered stairs on the right side and odd on the left.

A fake, twelve-foot Douglas fir tree decorated in silver and blue graced the downstairs dining room. Silver sleigh shaped candle holders with royal blue candles in them were placed on the tables as centerpieces. For the holiday season, blue cloth napkins would be used in the lower dining room to match the décor.

The waiting area adjacent to the Seashell Giving Tree had holly shaped candle holders with red candles placed on the tables. Silk poinsettia plants were placed randomly around the room.

Pine boughs and holly framed the front door with small red glass ornaments scattered throughout. A light dusting of fake snow finished the look. A pine wreath with matching red ornaments and flocked snow hung in the middle of the door.

They would decorate the bar and the upstairs dining room the following morning.

Jay unlocked the door at eleven and took up his post at the hostess station. It wasn't long before the customers started to enter, and Jay kept busy seating and socializing with his patrons.

The café owner received many compliments on his Christmas decorations. He gave all the credit to his mother and joked that she could do wonders when spending someone else's money.

Sheriff Boyd and his wife came for brunch. Jay seated them near the window that overlooked the ocean.

"Where are the boys?" Jay asked while he filled their water glasses.

"At Grandma's house," his wife answered, picking up the menu that placed in front of her. "We decided to treat ourselves and go out to eat."

"Enjoy your freedom. Maria will be over to take your order shortly," Jay said.

"Jay, can I talk to you for a minute?" Boyd asked.

"Sure, what's up?"

"Over here," Boyd instructed.

"Everything okay?" Jay asked when they were far enough away from his wife to speak.

"We found Ross Morris's car this morning down on Trace Point. There was blood in the back seat but no body. The keys were in the ignition and Morris's wallet was left on the front seat," Boyd stated.

"Did anyone see it pull into the point?" Jay inquired.

"No, it was dumped sometime during the early morning hours. The park rangers made rounds around midnight, and it wasn't there."

"Do you think it's a smokescreen? Maybe he wants people to think he's dead so the police will stop looking for him," Jay suggested.

"I don't know."

"Stephen, you promised you wouldn't bring your work with you to lunch," his wife announced. "You promised."

"I have to go. I did make that promise to her," the chief confirmed. "I'll talk to you tomorrow."

Jay returned to the front door. Business had slowed down, so he decided to get a Sunday paper out of the vending machine that was just outside the front door. He was feeding the quarters into the slot when he heard the rumble of machinery coming from the cottage construction site area.

That's strange. They've never worked on Sunday before, he thought, shielding his eyes from the sun and looking in that direction.

He couldn't see anything moving, and the noise stopped. Jay watched to see if anyone drove down from the site, but after a few minutes of seeing no one, he returned inside with the paper. He spread the paper out on the hostess station and was reading the front page when Bill Swann walked into the café.

"Bill, how's it going? Were you just up at my mom's cottage?"

"Yes, I was. They are coming tomorrow to start the stone wall in front of the tunnel area, and I marked out where the wall needs to go," he replied.

"I heard a backhoe running," Jay stated.

"I had to fill in the collapsed area," Bill explained. "Sometimes, you have to bury things so you can start over again."

"So are you here to eat?" Jay inquired.

"I am, and I am also here to get my shell. Talk around town is people are stepping up, and the shells are disappearing quickly," Bill commented.

"We have done really well so far. The giving tree has been up for less than a week, and already thirty-seven shells have been claimed. Do you have any preference? A single child, boy or girl, or a family?" Jay asked.

"I will sign up for whatever you need," Bill replied.

"Seriously? We have a real need for people signing up for families," Jay said. "There is a family of five that the dad has been out of work due to a car accident. Would you be willing to sponsor them?"

"Give me the info. My construction business has done outstanding this year and if you find yourself coming close to Christmas and you still need help, call me."

"Thanks, Bill. And the parents of the family you are helping thank you. Lunch is on me," Jay insisted.

"Lead me to the food," Bill said, smiling.

Jay seated Bill next to Roland's telescope, knowing if the ghost popped in to look out over the ocean, it wouldn't bother Bill. He sat by himself, looking out over the water while waiting for his food. His cell phone rang several times while he ate, which he answered each time. He was a busy man that didn't slow down just because it was Sunday.

Bill Swann never married. He had put all his time into building his business since he had graduated high school. The hard effort had paid off, and now he had one of the largest construction companies on the Cape and one of the most respected.

Jay had printed out signs to tell customers the café would be closed for Thanksgiving so his staff could celebrate at home with family. He was taping the signs to the windows and the front door when Kathy came in for work.

"Hey, boss, how was lunch?"

"Steady, but not crazy busy," Jay replied. "Mostly the local church crowd."

"So have you heard the latest gossip going around town?" Kathy asked.

"I don't spend a lot of time in town, so you know I haven't. If it doesn't involve my name, I don't need to know," he stated.

"Okay, so I guess that you don't want to know that Sid Swann left no will and with Emmaline dead too, their multi-million-dollar estate is in limbo…but…," Kathy paused for the dramatic effect.

"I'll bite. But what?" He smiled.

"Emmaline secretly had her own will drawn up and left everything to her son," Kathy squealed.

"But the Swann's had no children," Jay replied.

"Exactly!" Kathy said. "So who is this son named in her will?"

"Interesting. I wonder if Sid knew about him?"

"I bet he did and that's why Emmaline wouldn't leave him. Maybe he threatened her son," Kathy surmised.

"Who is this son? What's his name?" Jay asked.

"I thought that you weren't interested in local gossip?" Kathy teased. "The answer to your question is his name hasn't been released by Emmaline's attorney. They are trying to locate him first."

"This throws a new twist on the murders. Maybe he killed them for the inheritance," Jay stated.

"Maybe. Word is he was adopted and doesn't know who his real parents are."

"You sure learn a lot at church. Maybe I should start going." Jay laughed.

"It wouldn't hurt you," Kathy said, hanging up her coat next to the podium.

"Wait! Are you saying I am a bad person and should go to church?" Jay asked, holding his hand over his heart like he had been wounded.

"Not saying a word." Kathy smiled, heading for the kitchen.

I like her...

"I do too, my friend," Jay whispered as two patrons were leaving through the front door and he didn't want to be seen talking to himself.

She's spunky... Gives you a run for your money...

Yes, she does," Jay admitted.

How is Susan?

"She is still in the hospital. The doctors want to keep an eye on her a while longer. She might be able to come home tomorrow," Jay answered.

Did you dig up the well?

"No, I didn't. Not yet, anyway."

The treasure is not in the well... It is under the lighthouse.

"Why are you telling me this?"

I am not a liar... he insisted as he shimmered out of sight.

Kathy returned from the kitchen and took over the hosting duties from Jay. Free for the rest of the afternoon and night, he decided to go down to the Tunnel of Ships to check on the progress that was being made.

Jay had hired electricians to install track lighting along the entire passageway. This way, the museum could remain open into the evening hours and not have to depend on outside sunlight. A switch had been placed at the secret opening in the cellar and on the other end near the door that led to the outside.

He stood looking at the wooden tables installed along the plexiglass walls. They were empty right now but would soon have the information of every item in the tunnel placed on their surfaces.

Jay picked up the emerald hair comb. Instantly, a woman's sobbing reverberated throughout the tunnel.

"Who are you?" Jay asked. "I can hear you. Please tell me how to help you."

The noise grew louder. A faint 'help me' could be heard amongst the sobbing.

"How can I help you?" Jay repeated.

Drowning... Can't get out.

And then all went quiet.

"I guess my next step is to try to find out how this hair comb got into the tunnel. If Roland didn't know anything about it, who put it here?" Jay pondered. "But first, I need to take it to a jeweler and see if these emeralds are real or not."

He tucked the item into his coat pocket and exited the tunnel, turning the lights off behind him. As he closed the secret door, he heard the desperate plea for help again.

He locked the comb in the safe in his office intending to visit the local jeweler early the next morning. He said goodbye to Kathy, and after checking on Mandy in the kitchen, he headed home.

Martha had gone out for Sunday night bingo, so Jay had to cook for himself. He fired up the propane grill out on the deck and threw on a two-inch thick steak. While it cooked, he fixed a tossed salad as a side dish. The dogs waited patiently for their supper, but when Jay fed them, they were more interested in the meat that was cooking on the grill.

He ate supper, cleaned up after himself and then took a fresh beer into the living room. Jay built a fire, and the dogs settled in on their pillows in front of the hearth. Jay sat on the couch staring into the flames. He was glad he had returned to the Cape. Offseason life was the best. He closed his eyes and relaxed.

Someone knocked on the front door, and the dogs went crazy barking. He told them to be quiet and stay as he opened the door. Sheriff Boyd was waiting to be let in.

"Stephen! Don't tell me, more bad news?" Jay asked, standing aside so he could come in.

"No, not tonight. I came to return Roland's journal to you. It was released from evidence last Friday once the trial was completed. Redmond Jules will be spending the rest of his life in prison, no chance of parole," Boyd said, handing over the journal.

"Couldn't have happened to a nicer person," Jay stated. "What about Theresa?"

"Her trial starts next month," Boyd answered, giving Angie and Pickles a pat. "Well, I have to run. I have the night shift and a ton of paperwork to rummage through."

"Before you go, did you hear the latest gossip about Emmaline Swann having a secret son?" Jay inquired.

"Yea, and we are checking on it. Her attorney is tight-lipped about any information regarding him, so we are waiting for a court order to be issued for him to release his files."

"Do you think Emmaline told her son that he would inherit everything, and he killed them for the money? The estate is a sizable one."

"At this point anything is possible," Boyd admitted. "This case is driving me crazy. Nothing is leading to a solution."

"Something will break," Jay said, opening the door for the sheriff.

"I sure hope so. Bye, girls. Be good, dogs," Boyd said, closing the door behind him.

After getting another beer, Jay sat down and browsed through the journal that had just been returned to him. It had been out of his possession for several months, and he was glad to get it back. Now that business had slowed down, and he was only working three nights a week, he had some extra time to read the journal page by page and look for clues to the location of the treasure.

He opened the hidden safe in the living room and deposited the journal inside. He picked up the gold watch in the safe and turned it over in his hand. He popped open the watch and stared at the now stopped hands.

Roland said that this held the answer to the location of the treasure. There has to be a hidden compartment located somewhere in the watch, Jay thought.

He set it back into the safe and secured the door. Tossing the empty beer bottles into the recycling bin in the kitchen, he was heading upstairs with the dogs when Martha returned home from bingo.

"Did you win anything?" Jay asked.

"Not a thing," she answered. "Theresa won four times. She has got to be one of the luckiest people I know."

"How's her daughter doing?"

"She's done with the chemo and now only time will tell. She seems to be doing fine," Martha replied. "I'm heading to bed. I need to go to work early to make extra batches of chowder. Kathy informed me we have two tour buses coming in for lunch tomorrow."

"I told her I'd be in to help. I have a few errands to run before I go in. Maybe we can finish decorating the second floor on Tuesday morning?"

"Sounds good to me," Martha smiled. "I'll see you at lunch."

The house fell into total darkness, and its inhabitants slept peacefully. Outside the cottage, a figure took out a can of red spray paint and scrawled the word 'murderer' along both sides of Jay's car. The person laughed hysterically as they disappeared into the night.

14

*J*ay grabbed his coffee mug and opened the door to let the dogs out. A red-tailed hawk had been scoping out the area the last few days for his next meal and Pickles was small enough to be carted away in the hawk's talons. Jay had to stay close to the puppy to keep it from happening. He followed her around the corner of his cottage and spotted his vandalized car. His blood pressure rising, he pulled out his phone and dialed the sheriff.

Two cruisers sped up the hill, stopping next to Jay's car.

"You can't stay out of trouble, can you?" Sheriff Boyd said, climbing out of his vehicle. "I was just on my way home."

"Any idea who did it?" Deputy Nickerson asked.

"I have a really good idea," Jay claimed.

"Nickerson, take pictures of both sides of the car and check for footprints and tire prints around the area. Take pictures of anything you find," Boyd ordered. "So, who do you think is responsible for this?"

"I think it was Greg Peterson or his sister," Jay stated confidently.

"I know they are furious with you, but why do you think it was them?" Boyd asked.

"At the meeting of the reading of the will both stated that when I was convicted of murder, they would go after the return of the estate. Once the retraction printed in the paper, things died down and people accepted the fact that I was innocent. I think this is their way of keeping it fresh in the local's minds," Jay explained.

"Make's sense," Nickerson replied.

"We'll check it out. If it is him, do you want to press charges?" Boyd asked.

"I sure do. I don't think this paint is going to come off. The whole car will need to be repainted, and I want him or his insurance company to pay for it. The car is only two years old," Jay replied.

"I don't think it would do much good to dust for fingerprints," Nickerson said, returning the camera to his cruiser.

"I agree," Boyd said. "We'll be in touch when we know anything."

"I guess I'll have to hoof it to town," Jay stated. "I didn't do much jogging this summer. Time to start up again."

"I could use some jogging myself." Boyd, chuckled, wiggling his mid area.

"Come on, girls, in the house," Jay yelled to the dogs.

Martha came out the front door heading to the café. She spotted the car the same instant the dogs jumped up on her and almost knocked her over.

"Jay, what happened?" she asked, pushing the dogs down off her.

"We had a visitor in the middle of the night," Jay announced. "Nice, huh?"

"Who would do this?"

"I have my suspicions. I may need to borrow your car later," Jay replied.

"That's fine. Theresa and I are going off-Cape to do some shopping in Plymouth. The extra set of keys are on the hanger in the kitchen. She's picking me up from work, and we are eating supper somewhere up there."

"Have fun. I'll see you at the café before you leave," Jay said, herding the dogs inside to feed them.

Upstairs, he changed into a new sweat suit that he had bought in the spring and never used. He threw on an extra sweatshirt that had a zippered pocket in the front and followed right behind his mother to the café to pick up the emerald comb out of the office safe.

Secured in his zippered pocket, Jay stretched out and headed down the hill toward town. It felt good to be out running again. Usually, he ran on the beach, but there was little traffic on the roads as the tourists were gone and the locals were all at work.

Out of breath, he stopped in front of Anchor Point Jewelers that was just opening. He calmed his breathing and then entered the store. Phil Cook, the owner, stood behind a glass case at the rear of the sales floor. He was a third-generation jeweler and now owned the store that had been started by his grandfather eighty years ago.

"Phil, good to see you again," Jay said, offering an extended hand.

"Jay Hallett, I heard you had returned. Same Jay as in high school, still getting into trouble around town.," He laughed.

"Your mother always said that trouble was my middle name," Jay admitted. "How is she?"

"She's retired from teaching. She and Dad go to Florida for the winter and come back in June to spend the summers here."

"Nice. Do you have a few minutes to tell me if an item that I found is the real thing or just costume jewelry?" Jay requested.

"Sure, do you have it with you?"

"I do," Jay answered, unzipping his pocket and handing the hair comb to the jeweler.

Cook took out his eyepiece and examined the gems. He paid particular attention to the largest emerald set in the middle of the comb. Turning it over, he checked the piece for a maker's mark.

"Where did you get this?" he asked Jay.

"I found it buried in the dirt in my cellar. Why?"

"I'll be right back."

Cook returned from his office holding a pamphlet from a jeweler's convention held in Boston. He opened it to a page that displayed eight pieces, all done in emeralds. One of the items was identical to the hair comb that Jay had in his possession.

"Are you telling me that this piece is genuine? And a piece from this collection?"

"In 1869, the Duke of Alton commissioned a collection of emerald jewelry to be made as a wedding present for his new wife. Unfortunately, his new wife had been betrothed to another man, and she had ignored her father's wishes and married the Duke of Alton in secret. The jilted duke raided the castle where his supposed wife was living with her new husband. The Duke of Alton was murdered, but the wife was spared."

"Seriously? How did it get over here?" Jay inquired.

"She was forced into marriage with the man who killed her true love. They had a daughter, Lady Colletta. Duchess Sophia learned from her handmaiden that her husband was making advances on their own daughter, even though she was only nine years old. She decided to take her daughter and flee the country to somewhere far beyond her husband's reach. She gathered her emerald jewelry that she had kept secret from her second husband and as many gold and silver coins as she could lay her hands on without getting caught."

"How did she get out of the castle?"

"Sophia drugged her husband's nightcap with sleeping powder. When she knew he was out, she gathered her daughter and a leather satchel that held everything they would bring to the New World with them. They walked, under cover of the night, to get to the wharf to purchase passage on one of the ships leaving on the morning's high tide."

"Obviously, they made it onto a ship," Jay stated.

"Yes. Duchess Sophia and her daughter, Lady Colletta boarded *The Fallen Mist* and left for New York. She changed their names to Colleen and Sophie O'Mara so her husband couldn't track them."

Jay perked up when he heard the name Colleen O'Mara. Could it be possible that the ghost that roamed the point calling out for her mother could really be Lady Colletta of Alton? Could the sobbing ghost be Duchess Sophia?

"You know *The Fallen Mist* never made it to New York. It crashed out on the point in the worst storm of the century. They say there were no survivors. It was assumed that the satchel of emeralds sunk with the ship out in the ocean."

"Why is this so important now?" Jay asked.

"It is the one-hundred-and-fifty-year anniversary of the commissioning of the bridal set. In today's market, the eight emerald items would be valued at approximately twenty million dollars. No one knows how many gold and silver coins were in the satchel along with the jewelry. There is talk that a dive team is going to search for the wreck and the emeralds in the spring."

"So how did this end up in my cellar?" Jay wondered aloud.

"Good question. The better question would be is the rest of the pieces somewhere near where this one was located?" Cook replied.

"Tell me, what do you think this piece is valued at?" Jay asked.

"This is one of the smaller pieces. I would still value it at fifty thousand, maybe more because of the large center emerald. The historical find itself is priceless. This is proof that Duchess Sophia had to be on the ship when it wrecked," Cook said.

"You have to keep this quiet, Phil. I can't have my property overrun by press and treasure hunters again. I'll tell you what. If you don't tell anyone about the comb, if I find the rest of the collection, we will display it in your store for July Fourth weekend. People will visit from all over to see it, and that should be great for your business," Jay requested. "What do you say? Do we have an agreement?"

"You would display the emeralds in my store? Pictures of the interior of my store would be seen all over the world." Phil smiled. "You got a deal."

"Thank you. Now, I have to go lock this baby up for safekeeping," Jay commented, placing the comb in his pocket. "Remember, not a word."

Jay jogged home at a slower pace. It was all uphill to his house, and he was feeling it in his muscles when he arrived at the cottage. The very first thing he did was to put the emerald comb into the safe. He let the dogs out, and they ran straight to Colleen who was waiting to play with them. Jay stood on the deck and decided to test his theory.

"Lady Colletta," he yelled out.

The young ghost stared at Jay, a look of fear crossed her face, and she disappeared.

"I was right," Jay announced to the dogs as they returned to the deck. "Colleen is Lady Colletta."

Jay gave the dogs treats, and they followed him upstairs to lounge on the bed while their owner took a shower. He dressed for work but brought jeans and a flannel shirt with him to change into so that he could go down to the Tunnel of Ships when he was done working lunch.

The two tour buses pulled up at the same time, and eighty people were seated for lunch. It was hectic, and Jay wished he had asked an extra waitress to come in. The staff got through the rush okay and little by little, the diners left the building to walk around outside and enjoy the ocean views before they boarded the buses again to leave.

Jay changed in his office. When he opened the cellar door, the crying started immediately. He knew he had to help the ghost and get her and her daughter back together again. He had to take a chance and address her by her real name.

Drowning...

"Duchess Sophia, I know who you are, and I want to help you," Jay yelled over the noise.

The tunnel became silent. Jay waited to see if she would speak to him, but nothing.

"I need to know where you are. Where did you die? I can reunite you with your daughter, Lady Colletta if you let me help you."

Still nothing. Jay was afraid that he had scared the ghost and now he might never be able to help her. He sat in the dirt and waited another half hour, but to no avail. Total silence was the only thing that greeted him as he sat there.

Why are you sitting in the dirt?

"Oh, hi, Roland. I know who the crying ghost is, and I tried to talk to her. I called her by name, and she became silent. You will be happy to know that she is Colleen's mother, or should I say Lady Colletta's mother," Jay replied, standing up and brushing the dirt off his jeans. "The wailing ghost is Duchess Sophia of Alton."

Different names...

"Her mother changed their names to protect them from an abusive husband and father back in Spain. The had traveled on *The Fallen Mist* with the intention of starting a new life in New York when the ship hit its final port," Jay explained.

Her mother was alive when she made it to shore?

"I don't know that. We have to find where her body is buried."

I will check the tunnels...

"Good idea."

How do you know all this?

"The emerald hair comb was part of a set given to the duchess as a wedding gift from her first husband. She brought the emeralds with her to sell to start their new life in America."

I did not miss the body on the shore...

"No, my friend, I don't think you did. I think she wandered up onto the point looking for her daughter and something happened to her," Jay replied.

We must find her...for Colleen.

Roland faded away, and the tunnel became silent again.

"I'll be back to talk to you. I know where your daughter is, and she is looking for you. You must trust me. Your husband is long dead and cannot hurt either of you ever again. Please, give me some kind of clue as to where you died," Jay pleaded.

A voice spoke, clear as a bell.

Drowning... dark... Can't climb out...rocks.

"Are you in a cave near the water?"

No... Away from the ocean.

"Did you make it to town? Were you trapped in an underground tunnel?" Jay continued.

Can't hold on any longer... drowning.

"Lady Sophia, where did you drown?" Jay asked.

Silence.

"Lady Sophia, are you still here?"

Silence again.

"I'll be back," Jay announced as he shut the lights off in the tunnel.

His cell phone rang as soon as he reached the main cellar where reception was enabled again. The call was coming from the hospital. He answered knowing it was Susan.

"Hello."

"Hey, boss. You said to call when I knew anything. They are releasing me tomorrow morning," Susan said, cheerfully.

"What time do you want me there?" Jay asked.

"The doctor said that I should be out by eleven. Can you be here around then?"

"I'll be there. Mom wants to know if you will be okay to stay by yourself when you get out or if you want her to come and stay with you for a few days."

"Tell her I'll be fine, but thank her for the offer," Susan replied. "Hey, did the sheriff check out Ross Morris?"

"Yeah, he's disappeared."

"Interesting," Susan mumbled.

"I'll tell you all that I have learned when I pick you up tomorrow."

"Great! I'll see you then, and Jay? Thanks," she said.

Before he could respond, the line went dead. He had the night off and decided to do some research online to find out all he could about the duchess and her daughter. He appropriated some bay scallops from the walk-in along with some salad fixings that had come in fresh on that day's delivery.

Perks. He smiled as he walked out the back door onto the loading dock.

Taking out a casserole dish, he mixed some of the small, sweet scallops with butter, garlic, and white wine. He topped it off with Italian breadcrumbs and placed it in the oven to bake for twenty minutes.

Jay took the dogs out before it was completely dark, and the coyotes would be out on patrol for food. He looked around for Colleen while keeping an eye on the dogs. They weren't out long when they returned to the deck wanting their supper.

The dog's noses were sniffing the air when Jay removed his supper from the oven. He set the hot dish on a potholder on the table and set his salad next to his plate. The dogs, resigned to the fact they weren't going to get any of their master's scallops, returned to their own supper and cleaned their bowls.

As he ate, he searched online for articles referring to Duchess Sophia and Lady Colletta. He found black and white pictures of the mother and daughter on a European historical website.

The duchess was a stern looking woman. She had high-set cheekbones, and dark hair pulled back in a tight bun. Her eyes were piercing and could look right through to your soul. Around her neck, she wore the stunning emerald necklace that had been gifted to her. It was one of the pieces that Jay had seen in the picture Cook showed him.

Her daughter hadn't changed. The ghost on the point looked just like Lady Colletta when she lived in Spain. The only difference was the casual clothes the ghost had on for their trip across the ocean instead of the fancy dress in the picture.

Jay printed out all the research he had gathered. If he did find the rest of the emeralds, he wanted to be able to supply the IRS with everything he knew about the owners and where the jewels came from. He locked the papers in the safe with the comb.

He was cleaning up the kitchen when his cell rang.

"Stephen, what's up?" Jay asked the sheriff.

"I wanted to let you know that we questioned Greg Peterson and his sister about your car. They both swear they had nothing to do with the vandalism. They even let us check their garages, houses, and cars without getting a warrant. I don't think they did it," the sheriff announced. "Can you think of anyone else?"

"Could they have hired someone else to do?" Jay asked.

"Possibly, but unless that person starts running their mouth that they did it and someone hears them, it will be hard to prove," the sheriff confirmed.

"I can't think of anyone else who would do it," Jay replied.

"Give me a call if you do," the sheriff requested. "Bye."

Jay tossed and turned in bed. His mind wouldn't shut down so he could drift off to sleep.

I searched the tunnels...

Roland was standing next to Jay's bed. He was almost totally transparent as he floated in the air. Jay had never seen the ghost in this condition before.

"Roland, are you all right?"

Weak… searched all day and found nothing.

"Go rest, Roland. We will find her, I promise," Jay said, closing his eyes.

I'll be in the lighthouse…

Jay was asleep before Martha returned home from Plymouth.

15

*E*arly the next morning, Jay and Martha were busy decorating the second floor of the café for Christmas. Roland and Martha had decided together that the color scheme would be done in purples and silvers. The ghost was back to his old self and continued to pop in and out while the decorating took place.

Just before eleven, Jay left for the hospital to pick up Susan. He waited in the lobby until they brought her down in a wheelchair.

"I can't believe I had to ride in this stupid thing," she said, slowly standing up and climbing out of the chair.

"Susan needs a couple of prescriptions filled on the way home," the nurse told Jay. "And no work. Not until she is cleared by the doctor."

"She is going to spend the next couple of weeks at home, relaxing and doing nothing," Jay informed the nurse. "Except for Thanksgiving. I will be picking her up, and she will be at my house, still doing nothing except for eating."

Holding her ribs, Susan slowly lowered herself into Jay's car. She reached for the seatbelt and let out a small moan.

"Let me," Jay insisted, pulling the belt around her and snapping it into place.

"I feel like such a baby," she complained as Jay closed the door.

"Onward, James!" she laughed as he slid into the driver's seat. "Oh, no laughing. It hurts too much."

Jay drove her to the local pharmacy and then home. He made sure she was comfortable and had something to eat in the house. He brought down all her bed pillows so she could lay propped up on the couch to watch television.

"Don't you look like the queen?" he joked.

"No laughing, remember," she replied.

"Seriously, I'm glad you're okay," Jay said, moving the coffee table closer to the couch.

"I'll be fine after a little more rest. I want to get back to work as soon as possible," Susan said. "Holidays are coming up, and the café will be busy. Besides, I haven't done a lick of Christmas shopping yet."

"Come to think of it, I haven't either," Jay admitted.

"Maybe… we could go shopping together?" Susan asked, quietly.

"Sounds like a great idea. I can carry all the bags while you spend money," Jay teased.

"You're bad," Susan said. "I'll carry my own bags, thank you."

"I have to get back to work. I'm on the lunch shift which has already started. Good thing I'm the boss." Jay chuckled. "Call me if you need anything."

He put on his coat and was ready to leave. She smiled, leaned back, and closed her eyes. Jay had never noticed how pretty Susan was until that moment. She was always just another cook behind the line. Yes, they would go Christmas shopping and maybe for dinner. And he would definitely think about asking her to be his date for the Christmas Ball.

MARTHA HAD FINISHED DECORATING the upstairs and lunch was in full swing when Jay returned. She was helping Kathy seat people until Jay showed up for work. He came through the front door whistling. Both Kathy and Martha noticed.

"Well, someone is in a good mood," Martha said, smiling at her son. "Is Susan okay?"

"She's at home, lounging like a queen on her couch," Jay answered.

"Did she say when she could come back to work?" Martha asked.

"Not for another couple of weeks anyway. I did invite her to have Thanksgiving dinner with us," Jay admitted. "She can't drive the long distance to her sister's house, and she has no one else in the area."

"I'm sure that's the only reason," Kathy snickered as she walked away.

"And what's that supposed to mean?" Jay inquired, crossing his arms in front of his chest.

Martha threw her hands up in the air.

"I'm going home," she said, grabbing her coat and leaving through the front door before Jay could say another word.

In between seating customers, Jay and Kathy wrapped different size boxes that would hold the donated gifts around the tree. Each box had a Christmas tag adhered to it with a corresponding number on the list. The wrapped, empty boxes would stay in Jay's office until gifts were placed in them and added under the giving tree out front.

Sixty-seven shells had already been claimed. Some locals had already returned the gifts they bought and taken another shell. Jay was totally confident that every boy, girl, and family would be taken care of for Christmas. And the ones that were left on the tree, if any, would be taken care of by himself, Robbie, and Martha. By the night of the Seashell Christmas Ball, the giving tree would be covered with only angels and no shells.

ROBBIE HAD GONE to North Carolina on vacation for two weeks with a couple of his friends. He would be home the day before Thanksgiving. Martha's new cottage was nearing completion, ahead of schedule.

There had been no breaks in either murder case, and Ross Morris was still missing. Jay's car had been repainted a royal blue to cover the vandalism done to it. No one was held accountable yet for the damage.

He had visited Susan, checking on her and taking her to doctor's appointments. The month of November had passed quickly, and Thanksgiving Day had arrived.

Martha was up early stuffing the turkey and preparing the side dishes. She had baked four pies the day before and had apple cider and eggnog chilling out on the deck. The captain's table in the kitchen was set for dinner and the wine chilling in the refrigerator. The dogs were running around the kitchen snagging anything that fell to the floor.

"Smells great in here," Jay said, entering the kitchen.

"Dinner will be ready at one. Make sure you have Susan here before then. Oh, and I asked Bill Swann to join us. He has no family left now, and I didn't want him to be alone," Martha stated. "He should be here around noonish."

"I told Susan I would pick her up at noon. She's moving around a lot better now and should be able to come back to work soon," Jay replied.

"That's great news, not that Brian isn't doing a wonderful job running the kitchen," Martha said. "You were lucky he could step right in and take over."

"I am lucky. I have a staff that any owner would kill for," Jay said, stealing a stuffed fig rolled in sugar.

"Go do something. Get out of my kitchen if you are going to steal food and not help," Martha ordered.

"Yes, ma'am," Jay answered, smiling that his mother felt so at home living with him that she called it her kitchen. "I'll be in the living room checking out what football games are on today."

"And take these dogs with you," she added.

Jay started a fire. He hoped that maybe later he could ask Susan to go to the ball with him while sitting on the hearth enjoying a glass of wine. And it helped to warm up the drafty cottage against the winter winds that blew off the water. He flipped on the television and searched the guide for games on later in the day.

Jay dozed off in front of the warm fire. A knock on the front door started the dogs barking, waking him up. He told them to be quiet and answered the door. Bill Swann was holding several bottles of wine in one arm and balancing a cheese tray on the other.

"Let me help," Jay said, grabbing the cheese tray. "Is it noon already? I can't believe I dozed off. Mom, Bill is here," Jay announced leading him to the kitchen. "I have to go get Susan, and I am late."

"I thought you had already left since it was so quiet in there," Martha stated.

"I fell asleep."

"Now why doesn't that surprise me?" she replied. "Go! Go get Susan. Dinner is in less than an hour."

"I'll be right back. Robbie texted me and told me he'd be here at twelve-thirty."

Twenty minutes later, Jay arrived back at the house with Susan. She was dressed in black slacks, a white blouse, and a vest with turkeys holding different cooking utensils scattered over it. She walked into the kitchen and gave Martha a big hug. Susan had baked brownies, apple crisp, and assorted cookies to contribute to the festivities. Jay had carried in the sweets and set them on the dessert table alongside the pies.

"What can I do to help?" Susan asked.

"You can take yourself into the living room with Jay and Bill until I call you all for dinner," Martha answered, stirring the gravy on the stovetop.

"Let me know when you want the turkey to come out of the oven," Jay told his mom.

"Shortly, now go, all of you."

Jay poured everyone a glass of wine. They had just sat down when Robbie came through the front door. His contribution was a bottle of expensive cognac for later in the evening. He went into the kitchen to say hi to their mom and then returned to the living room.

"She threw me out of the kitchen. She hasn't seen me for two weeks, and she threw me out," he said, opening a beer that he grabbed out of the fridge in the kitchen.

"She threw us all out." Bill laughed.

Robbie joined the others in front of the fireplace. Susan announced the doctors gave her the all clear to return to work with a few restrictions. Jay asked Bill about the progress of his mom's cottage, and Bill assured him she would be in her new home before Christmas. The conversation turned to the giving tree and the ball just as Martha called her son to come help her with the turkey.

Roland popped in as Jay was placing the turkey on a tray for carving. *That looks good…*

"Yes, it does. My mom cooks a tasty turkey," Jay agreed.

I miss food… the smells.

"I wish there were some way you could join us," Martha told the ghost.

I will be here in spirit…

He shimmered away as Robbie entered the kitchen.

"Was that Roland?"

"Yeah, he misses eating food," Jay answered.

"I think I would miss that the most, too. Well, maybe beer and then food." Robbie laughed.

Everyone was called to the table. Martha said grace and the eating started. Robbie's plate was so full that the gravy flowed over the sides and onto the tablecloth. He managed to eat it all and went back for seconds while everyone else was still on firsts.

"So how are the ticket sales going for the ball?" Bill asked.

"Really well," Jay answered. "We have sold almost two hundred and fifty tickets so far, and the ball is still two weeks away."

"That is going to really help defray the costs of the new museum," Robbie stated.

"We may even begin to start on the renovations of the back building into a gift shop and additional museum space," Jay replied.

"And the giving tree is a huge hit. I think at last count there were only eight shells left on the tree. So many locals are pitching in this year to help others have a good Christmas," Martha added. "I hope the ones receiving the donated gifts appreciate all that is being done for them."

"I hope so. Some people don't appreciate anything, no matter what you do for them," Bill stated in a nasty tone of voice.

Everyone looked at Bill.

"Sorry, I was just thinking about my brother," Bill offered as a lame excuse for his tone of voice. "Anyway, I hear through the grapevine that

Phil Cook is going to run for my brother's selectman spot in the special election in January."

"I heard that, too," Martha commented. "I think he would make a fine selectman. He is very well liked and was born and raised here."

"Another rumor I heard floating around town is that Jay found a little bit of history here in Anchor Point," Bill stated.

"What do you mean?" Jay asked.

"Something about an emerald hair comb that belonged to a duchess from Spain. I can't remember what her name was offhand," Bill said.

"Yeah, Phil Cook would make a great politician. He can't be trusted when he gives his word on something." Jay scowled.

"Then it's true?" Bill inquired.

"I'm still looking into it," Jay muttered, mad that Phil ran his mouth about the find.

"Anyone want some coffee?" Martha asked, trying to change the conversation.

"I would love some coffee," Susan answered. "Jay, come help me so your mother can finish her meal."

"Don't let Bill get to you and ruin your mother's Thanksgiving. Forget about the hair comb, or whatever it is, and sit back down at the table with a smile," Susan whispered so no one else would hear her.

"You're right. Thanks. I sometimes forget what it means to live in a small town where everyone knows your business," Jay admitted, picking up the pot of coffee.

After pouring coffee for everyone at the table, Susan set the empty pot on the dessert table and sat down. The conversation remained light from that point on and no more mention of the comb.

"Take your coffee and go into the living room while I clear off the table," Martha suggested.

"No! You cook, I clean. That's the deal, remember? You go sit in front of the fire and enjoy yourself. You've been working all day," Jay said to his mom.

"But..."

"No buts. I will help Jay clean the kitchen. You have already done your fair share," Susan insisted.

"Okay," Martha finally agreed. "But only because I want to hear about Robbie's trip."

Jay and Susan got busy cleaning the kitchen. Working together, the dishes were done in no time, and the table reset for dessert. Jay refilled their wine glasses, and Susan started to walk toward the living room.

"Before we go back in there, can I ask you a question?"

"Sure, what is it?" Susan said, turning around.

"I was wondering if you would go to the Seashell Christmas Ball with me?"

"I'm sorry, but I can't. Brian asked me to go with him right before my accident," she answered. "I would love to have gone with you, but Brian asked me first."

"That's okay. I know you'll have a good time with Brian. He's a good guy," Jay replied, trying to hide his disappointment.

Susan turned to leave the kitchen.

"Hey, Jay, next year, don't wait so long to ask me," she said, walking through the door.

He smiled and joined the others in the living room. The rest of the day was spent watching football, laughing, and eating dessert. Bill left around six and offered to drop Susan off on the way. Robbie left shortly after the others, claiming he was still catching up on lost sleep from his vacation.

Jay dozed off again while listening to Martha and Roland bantering back and forth in the kitchen. He woke up sometime after eleven. His mother had already gone to bed. Going to the kitchen for a cold bottle of water to take with him upstairs, he swiped a chunk of turkey off the towel covered carcass in the fridge.

Another great Thanksgiving, and I am so glad that my mom was still here to celebrate it with us. And I am glad she decided to stay in Anchor Point.

Jay shut out the lights and headed for the stairs with the dogs in tow.

Goodnight, Jay...

"Goodnight, Roland. Happy Thanksgiving, my friend."

16

Over the next week, Jay and Susan went Christmas shopping together. Just like Jay predicted, Susan shopped, and he carried the bags. He picked up a few things here and there but was mostly giving gift cards to his family—a man's typical way out of shopping.

He did purchase a new tuxedo for the ball on one of their shopping trips. The one he had was outdated and reminded him of too many bad memories when living in Boston. He bought a bright red ruffled shirt, a green cummerbund, and new dress shoes to go with the tux.

Susan picked up her dress for the ball but wouldn't let Jay see it. She kept it hidden in its dress bag stating that no one would see it until the night of the ball. Jay teased her about it not being a bridal gown that had to stay secret, but she still wouldn't show him.

Two days before the ball, Jay and Kathy did an inventory of what gifts had been bought and returned to the giving tree and who still needed to drop off their donations. Just as Jay had wanted, the tree was covered in angels, and not a single shell remained.

Several reporters had wandered into the café looking for a story on the Duchess of Alton and the emerald hair comb. He turned them all away, but not until finding out that it was one of Phil Cook's clerks who leaked the story that she had overheard.

The day before and the day of the ball, the café was closed for business. Additional decorations and lighting had to be put up. Large, white, glitter-covered snowflakes of varying sizes were hung from the ceilings on both floors. Small spotlights were placed in inconspicuous areas around the café that would shine toward the ceiling to make the snowflakes glisten even more when they were moved by the central air-conditioning.

Tables were removed and a temporary dance floor set up in the center of the first-floor dining room. Tables along the perimeter of the room were for people who just wanted to sit and listen to the music.

The band would set up in the far corner of the room. The music could be heard upstairs, but not to the same degree of loudness. A large disco ball would bathe the dance floor and its surrounding area in small wandering glimmers of silver dots.

A U-shaped buffet table had been set up to the left of the bar. All the tables remained in place on the second floor for people to eat, sit, and socialize. There would be four bartenders operating the bar, three of which were outside hires so his employees could attend the ball.

A local catering company had full run of the café kitchen to cook the food. Stuffed mushrooms, scallops wrapped in bacon, shrimp cocktail, and many other finger foods were on the menu and would be offered right up until the ball ended at one.

The Seashell Giving Tree was surrounded by gifts. It would be the first thing that the attendees would see when they entered the café. It was a beautiful symbol of how the community had come together to help their own.

IT WAS the afternoon of the ball. Jay took the dogs out for an extra-long run knowing they would be at home all night by themselves. Colleen was standing out on the point searching for her mother. Jay had to figure out where she was buried. Once Christmas was over, he would have more time to figure it out.

It was three o'clock. Jay showered and donned his tux. He had to be over at the café by four to make sure everything was ready to go for the five o'clock opening. Kathy's sister had offered to stand at the door and check tickets. She knew Kathy wanted to attend the ball with her new boyfriend and show him off.

In the waiting area behind the giving tree, there were rented coat racks, and they had hired two hatcheck people to handle the large influx of coats.

When Jay arrived at four, the band was already sound checking their equipment and people were hustling around making sure all was finished and perfect. He stepped into the kitchen to check on the catering company and was met by the owner. She assured him everything would go smoothly and that she had enough food to feed an army.

He wandered up to the bar next. He was helping himself to a bourbon on the rocks when approached by one of the bartenders who told him that he couldn't be behind the bar and that it wasn't open yet. Pat, one of Jay's regular bartenders, hurried over to tell the young man who Jay was. The hire apologized to the owner and hurried off to the other end of the bar.

Jay returned downstairs to see his mother talking to Kathy's sister at the front door. He wished his dad could be here to see how beautiful his mom looked. Dressed in a green velvet, floor-length gown, her hair was dotted with silver crystals that sparkled when she moved. He walked up to his mom and gave her a hug.

"I have something for you," he said, reaching under the hostess station and bringing out a corsage box. "Dad would have got you this if he were here."

He pulled out a wrist corsage made up of red teacup roses and white baby's breath. A green bow that matched her dress perfectly finished the corsage's look. She held out her arm and Jay placed it on her wrist.

"It's beautiful, son," she said, tearing up. "I miss him, too."

"I need to run to the office and get the list of ticket sales. I'll be right back," Jay said.

He knew the list was on his desk somewhere, but where?

You look good…

"Roland, I need to apologize in advance. It's going to be very noisy here tonight with the band playing and all the people. I'm sorry, my friend, but it's for a good cause. The money raised here is going to fund your Tunnel of Ships and the new museum out in the back building," Jay explained.

Couldn't climb out...that's what she said.

"What are you talking about?" Jay asked, still searching for the list.

She wasn't near the shore, but she is drowning.

"Have you figured something out, Roland?"

She was on land, but she couldn't climb out.

"Ah, found it," Jay said, holding up the lost list. "I'll have to talk to you later. I need to get this to the front door as people are already arriving."

Jay hurried out of the office. Roland shrugged his shoulders and shimmered out. He decided to hide up in the lighthouse for the rest of the night.

Jay stayed at the front door greeting people as they arrived. After a while, he decided to make the rounds and get something to eat. He took his plate to the bar to get a drink. The same bartender who had questioned him earlier served him again.

"No charge, sir," he mumbled. "Enjoy your evening."

Jay snickered as he watched the bartender get as far away as he could from the end of the bar where Jay was sitting. Bill Swann sat down next to Jay.

"What a great turnout," he said. "This is like one of those high society balls that you would see in big city papers."

"I've never seen you in a tux," Jay commented.

"Rental," Bill said.

"Jay, the place looks great. I can't believe the number of gifts surrounding the Seashell Giving Tree. The locals really came through," Stephen Boyd said, standing next to Jay.

"Yes, they did," Jay agreed.

"Can I have a glass of white wine and a whiskey on the rocks," Stephen asked the bartender.

"Where's your wife?" Bill asked.

"She's downstairs with Martha being sociable." He laughed. "I'm just not the social type."

Jay looked over Bill's shoulder and spotted Susan and Brian arriving at the top of the stairs. Susan was dressed in a bright red satin ball gown with a floor-length green sash. Her hair had been curled and pinned up with soft curls falling around her face and neck. She looked stunning. Jay was regretting the fact that he hadn't asked her sooner.

"Earth to Jay," Boyd said, looking in the direction that Jay was staring. "Wow! She looks pretty good for having so many broken ribs."

"Yes, she does," Jay said, standing up.

"So, this is the secret dress?' Jay asked Susan, smiling.

"This is it," Susan said, twirling in a circle.

"Where is your crown?" Jay teased.

"I left it at home in my castle," she shot right back.

"Hello, Brian. Nice tux."

"Hello, sir... Jay, I mean."

"Enjoy the evening. Check out the food, it's pretty good. Susan, save a dance for your boss," Jay suggested as he walked away.

The phone rang behind the bar, and Pat answered it. She shook her head and hung up.

"Jay, they need you down at the front door. Something about tickets," Pat said to her boss.

"Pat, the next drinks for Stephen and Bill are on the house," Jay said.

"In that case, I'll have the good stuff, straight up," Stephen laughed.

Jay reached the front door to see a man and woman he didn't know arguing with Kathy's sister. They were rude and loud.

"Is there a problem here?" Jay asked.

"We bought these tickets at full price, and this woman is trying to tell us they are not real tickets," the lady complained loudly.

"May I see the tickets?"

Jay looked over the tickets, front and back. You could tell immediately that the tickets were copies made on a printer.

"Where did you buy these tickets?" Jay inquired, thinking to himself that they couldn't be that stupid.

"A man was selling them outside the Coffee Café. He had a whole bunch of them," the man insisted. "Other people bought them from him, too."

Kathy had wandered over to see what was going on.

"Kathy, do me a favor and call the bar to see if Stephen is still there. If he is, ask him to come to the front door, please," Jay requested.

The line of people waiting to enter was backing up out the door.

"Could you please step over here while we get this sorted out?" Jay suggested to the couple.

The sheriff joined them at the door, and Jay explained what was happening and showed him the fake tickets. Boyd questioned them about the person who sold the tickets to them and asked for as good a description as they could remember.

"I will honor these tickets because you were robbed using my name and business. I'd like to keep the tickets if you don't mind," Jay requested.

"Sure. I'm sorry we were so rude. We had no idea the tickets were fakes," the woman apologized.

"From what you said, there will be more showing up," Jay said, sliding the tickets into his tux pocket. "Have a nice evening."

"Do you know them?" Boyd asked.

"No, do you?"

"No. I've never seen them before tonight."

"Keep your eyes open for other fake tickets," Jay advised. "Call me if any more show up."

Jay and Stephen walked back to the bar. Martha and the chief's wife were waiting for them and talking to Bill. Martha wanted to know what was going on. Jay told them about the fake tickets.

"Some people will do anything for money," Bill commented. "Sad."

"It couldn't have been someone local, or they'd have been easily recognized," Jay surmised.

"Well, I for one..." Martha started to say.

"The well! That's what Roland was trying to tell me," Jay exclaimed, jumping up. "The duchess fell down the well and couldn't climb out."

"What are you talking about now?" Boyd asked.

"I have to dig up my mother's back yard to find the abandoned well. It is somewhere near the end of the tunnel that Bill discovered when he was working up at the new cottage," Jay explained. "We'll have to dig up the area again to find the tunnel and where it leads to."

While Jay was telling Boyd about the emerald comb, and the sobbing ghost attached to it, Bill Swann quietly slipped away from the bar.

"Bill, just how far did the tunnel run…" Jay asked, turning around. "Where did Bill go?"

"I don't know. He was here just a second ago," Martha replied.

"Are you talking about the man who was just sitting there?" the bartender asked, pointing to the empty chair.

"Yes, where did he go?" Jay asked.

"He got a really scared look on his face when you started talking about the well. He threw a twenty on the bar and took off down the stairs," he replied. "The funny thing is, he already paid his tab."

"Can we please just have a nice Christmas party without talking mysteries or murder?" Sheriff Boyd's wife complained.

"I second that," Martha said.

"Okay, boss, I'm here to claim that dance. Let's go. They are playing a nice slow song so my ribs won't kill me on the dance floor," Susan said, hooking her arm in his.

"I guess I am being kidnapped," Jay sighed. "Lead me to the dance floor."

The couple stayed to the side of the dance floor so that no one would bump Susan in the ribs. It was a slow dance and Jay pulled her in as close as he dared without hurting her.

"You look beautiful," Jay whispered.

"Thank you, and you look pretty good yourself," she whispered back.

"Remember when we were talking about the duchess and the emeralds when we were shopping. I think Roland figured out where she died."

"Where is she? Or should I say where is her body?" Susan asked.

"Roland thinks—or he hinted, anyway—he thinks she fell down the well and couldn't get back out. When I was in the tunnel, she said she couldn't climb out, and she mentioned rocks. Wells are usually lined with rocks."

"I didn't know there was a well on the property," Susan stated, laying her head on Jay's shoulder.

"It was filled in back in 1909 when a young boy fell in and drowned. They dug a tunnel to break into the side wall to drain it and to recover the child's body. Bill stumbled onto the tunnel when he was leveling the side yard at my mom's cottage to lay a driveway."

"Wouldn't they have found her bones when they drained the well?"

"She would have fallen in almost ten years prior and they only drained the well water low enough to find the child. Her bones and possibly the emeralds could have been in the mud under the remaining water."

"Are you going to dig up the tunnel again and hope it leads you to the well?

"That's the weird thing. I turned to ask Bill about the tunnel, and he had disappeared," Jay said. "The bartender said he was in such a hurry to get out of there he paid his tab twice."

"Do you think he is going to try to dig up the well himself to get the emeralds? Maybe he knew about her location before you did. Didn't you say he was up there on a Sunday, running equipment when no one else was around and that they never worked on Sunday before?" Susan questioned.

"Yes, I did. He said he was moving a pile of dirt because they were going to build a stone wall in front of the tunnel the next morning so no one else would fall in. But, come to think of it, the wall still hasn't been built," Jay stated. "I better dig out my thermals. I'm going to talk to the sheriff about sleeping at the work site the next few nights to see if Bill shows up," Jay replied.

"Maybe it will only be for one night if he shows up later tonight to try to beat you to the punch," Susan said. "If I didn't have these busted ribs, I'd stay with you. I love doing exciting stuff."

The music ended, and Brian was waiting on the side of the dance floor for his date.

"Let me know what happens," she requested as she left.

He watched her walk away with her date. As soon as she was feeling well enough to return to work, he would ask her to go out to dinner with him. She was pretty, had a great sense of humor, and a taste for adventure.

The single women lined up to dance with Jay over the next couple of hours. He needed a break to cool down and sat at the bar upstairs to get away from the dance floor area. He watched. He was a people watcher and always had been.

He was trying to figure out why Bill Swann ran out in such a hurry. He rehashed all the conversations he and the contractor had had in the last few months. Then it hit him. Jay had to find Sheriff Boyd.

"Are you sure?" Boyd asked Jay.

"Think about it, Stephen. It makes sense."

"I guess I need to go home and change. Sometimes I really hate this job. My wife is going to be so mad," Boyd stated. "She spent a fortune on her dress."

"If she wants to stay, I'm sure my mom would bring her home later," Jay offered.

"She won't stay if I'm not here. But we have to catch him in the act," Boyd confirmed. "I'll park my car at your place and walk up to the construction site. I'll meet you near the back door."

Jay found Robbie and Martha and told them he had to leave. He didn't go into detail but did tell them he had to go somewhere with the sheriff. It was already eleven o'clock, and the ball ended in two hours. He asked Robbie to stick around and close the café, and he said he would.

Jay left to go home and change. He met the sheriff a half an hour later. They sat just inside the sliders on the back deck of the house, wrapped in blankets, watching the dark area of the reburied tunnel.

17

*T*he lights had died down outside the café. The parking lot had turned into darkness as the last car left the ball. Both Jay and the sheriff dozed off here and there but woke up again when they heard any kind of noise. The sheriff stood up to stretch his legs. He quickly squatted down again and tapped Jay on the shoulder, pointing out into the darkness.

A figure was walking along the filled-in tunnel. A flashlight turned on and was partially covered with a hand to stifle the light. The figure walked along as if looking for a specific spot. He laid a tarp out on the ground and started to dig.

Jay and the chief continued to watch. They didn't want to stop him too early before they had the evidence they needed. He dug for almost an hour.

"He can't use the backhoe," Jay whispered. "This going to take a lot longer than he figured."

"Look," the sheriff whispered.

The figure had jumped down in the hole and was pushing something up and onto the tarp. Before he could climb out of the freshly dug ditch, the sheriff and Jay ran through the sliders and turned on their flashlights.

Bill threw his hands up in the air as soon as the flashlight beam lit up his face.

"Stay where you are, Bill," the sheriff ordered.

Jay walked around the hole to the tarp and shined the beam on what Bill was trying to move. The corpse had a tattoo on his forearm of two crossed hammers.

"I think we found the missing Ross Morris," Jay stated.

"Why, Bill? Why would you do this?" the sheriff asked.

"What does it matter now?' he answered.

"It does matter. It matters to everyone who lives in this town," Jay said.

"Remember how I said some people don't appreciate anything you do for them? Well, that's what happened to me. All the years I protected Emmaline from my brother, all the years I loved her more than my brother did, and the minute she is free from Sid, she latches on to him," Bill lamented. "I saw her kill her husband, my brother, and I still protected her and kept it secret."

So, you felt betrayed when you caught them in bed together and killed them both?" Boyd asked.

"No, no, that's not how it was. He killed my Emmaline. He killed her out of anger. She was going to tell him that he had just been a fling and that she was going to come back to me. We were going to find our son together. He flew into a rage. I was watching through the window. He jumped on top of her and put his hands around her throat," Bill sobbed. "By the time I found my key to the house and got inside, Emmaline was dead, and he was going through her purse looking for money."

"So you killed him?"

"I didn't know what I was doing. I was furious. He killed the mother of my child,' Bill confessed. "I didn't mean to kill him, I guess. I hit him with the lamp, and I think I hit him too hard. I just meant... I don't know what I meant.

"Emmaline's secret son is your son?" Jay asked. "Not Sid's?"

"Sid couldn't have children, but he never told Emmaline that. When she got pregnant, he knew the rumors were true that we were seeing each other behind his back. That's when the abuse started and when my son was born, he was put up for adoption. I never saw him, and neither did Emmaline. Sid told his wife that if she ever left him and hurt his reputation, she would never find out where her son—our son—had been adopted."

"That answers the question of why she never left Sid," Boyd replied.

So let me get this straight. Emmaline killed her husband, Ross killed Emmaline, and you killed Ross," Jay surmised.

"I think I want an attorney," Bill stated, nodding his head and staying silent from that point on.

Boyd called the on-duty deputy to come pick up the prisoner. Bill was handcuffed and sitting on the ground next to the corpse when the cruiser pulled up.

"Nickerson, when you get back to the station, call the coroner to come get the body," Boyd instructed. "I'll be in my cruiser at the front of the house waiting."

"Yes, sir. It shouldn't be more than an hour or so," Nickerson said.

"Jay, why don't you head home and get some sleep and warm up," Boyd suggested. "I'll need you to come to the station tomorrow to make a statement."

"I'll be there. Afternoon okay?"

Boyd nodded, and Jay left to go home. The sun was just peeking over the ocean's horizon, and the sky was splattered in pinks and blues. He crept quietly into the house and fell into bed exhausted. This time, he didn't even mind the fact the dogs weren't there.

He crawled out of bed shortly after noon. Martha was sitting in the living room when he came downstairs.

"It's all over town," she said. "Are you okay?"

"Yeah, I'm fine. Stephen and I had the jump on Bill. He fell apart the minute he knew he had been caught with Ross's body," Jay answered. "Where are the dogs?"

"Robbie took them out for a walk."

"How did it go last night?"

"Everything went fine. The café is closed today, so there is no rush to clean and reset," Martha said. "Robbie didn't get out of there until after three."

"I owe him big time. Is there any coffee?"

"You'll have to make a fresh pot," Martha said.

She is in the well…

"Jay figured out what you meant last night," Martha told Roland.

"Yes, I did. I'm sorry I was so rude to you in the office," Jay apologized.

You were busy… Can we help her?

"Yes, we can. I am going to go to the construction site in a little while and ask whoever it is that runs the backhoe to help me find the well. We may have to dig using shovels once we reach the bottom of the well so we don't destroy any bones we may uncover," Jay explained to the ghost. "It may take a while."

Today?

"Yes, today."

I will be watching…

18

*J*ay, Martha, and the sheriff stood at the back of the house watching the foreman dig up the tunnel that had been refilled. He yelled to Jay when he reached what he thought was a stone wall. Jay jumped down into the pit and examined the rocks. They had been placed in a circular shape—the shape of a well.

"I think we found it," Jay yelled. "I can't tell how deep it is, though."

"I can line up the teeth to the edge of the wall and pull the dirt back, going deeper but not inside the round rock formation," the foreman suggested.

"Okay, let's take it slow, though," Jay agreed, jumping out of the pit.

The backhoe started to dig again. After they had cleared just four shovels of dirt, Jay announced that the well wall had fallen apart, and they would have to dig manually from here on. He figured they were about thirty feet deep.

Boyd threw a shovel down to Jay. He started to remove the dirt from the inside of the well. A couple of times, he looked up and saw Roland standing at the edge of the pit, watching every shovel full of dirt Jay removed. After digging for a half an hour, Jay sat in the dirt to take a break. He leaned back to rest against the wall and felt something hard stick him in the back.

He turned to find a buckle half exposed in the dirt. Jay pulled it out.

"Did you find something?' Martha asked.

"A buckle. I can't tell what it went to, though," he answered.

He stood up again and continued shoveling. Several minutes later, when he tossed the dirt behind him, he heard a clink. He dropped to his knees and sifted through what he had just thrown there.

Did you find something?

Roland was standing next to him. He couldn't wait up above anymore and had joined Jay down in the pit.

"Coins," Jay answered. "People have always thrown coins into wells to make wishes. I bet they did back at the turn of the century, too."

Yes, they did…

"Finding the coins means we should be near or at the bottom of the well," Jay stated.

Dig…

Jay laid out a blue tarp that he had brought with him in case they found the bones. He scooped up the dirt from the last shovel-full and placed it on the tarp so that later he could find the old coins for the museum. As he turned to start shoveling again, a loud crying could be heard from the well area.

Keep digging. We are close…

The more dirt Jay removed, the louder the crying got. Now everyone, including the construction crew, could hear the noise emanating from the well. Jay dug with a renewed spirit that he must be getting close to Duchess Sophia's last resting place.

Jay hit something hard, and the crying stopped. He looked down at the dirt on the shovel and saw a small bone. He knew he had found her. He carefully laid the dirt and bone on the tarp. Jay turned to say something to Roland, but he was gone.

"I found her!" Jay yelled up to the now large group of people who were watching him dig. "At least I think it's her."

He didn't want to disturb the area too much. He poked around with a trowel he had been keeping in his back pocket. Along with more bones, he uncovered the top of a disintegrating metal box. Jay carefully dug out around it, but as he dug, the top of the box caved in. A bright green color reflected the sun that was shining on the box.

Jay stood the shovel against the well wall and dropped to his knees. He slowly pushed the remaining dirt away from the sides of the box. The more he moved things around, the more the box fell apart. He reached in and pulled out the most exquisite emerald necklace he had ever seen. He held it up for everyone to see.

"Jay, you found it! Roland was right," Martha exclaimed.

"Who's Roland?" a voice asked.

As he looked around the pit's edge, he noticed more people had come from town to watch. Two people, in particular, were taking a lot of pictures with their phones. Jay called the sheriff down into the pit. When they were done conversing, the sheriff rejoined the crowd that had gathered and walked over to the two people who were taking the pictures. The same two people who had presented fake tickets to get into the ball the previous night.

"Do you have some ID?' he asked.

"Why? We haven't done anything wrong," the man protested.

"You are on private property, uninvited," the sheriff answered. "IDs please."

"Oh, just tell him," the lady said.

"We are reporters from the Boston Sunrise. Word got to our paper that the jewels of Duchess Sophia might be found here, so our paper sent us to cover the story."

"Why the fake tickets last night?" Boyd asked.

"We needed to get into the ball to see if we could pick up any leads," the woman explained.

Jay had been listening from the pit.

"Tell them they owe us eighty dollars for the tickets," he yelled as he continued to pull the emerald collection, piece by piece, out of the ground.

Martha walked over and held out her hand.

"Fine, here's your money," the man said, taking out his wallet and putting four twenties in her hand.

"I think they need to leave. This is private property," Susan said, walking up to the group.

"I agree. Let's go, you two," the sheriff said, escorting them away from the area.

"Fine. We got a picture of the necklace and where she was buried," the man said. "We can figure out the rest of the story ourselves. But what was that noise we heard?"

Jay looked up, smiling at Susan. She was a feisty one. He admired that. He waved her down into the pit.

"Hold out your hands," he said.

She did, and he placed the emerald necklace in her hands.

"Jay, it's gorgeous," she said, catching her breath.

"I have all the pieces that were unaccounted for in the collection. The more important thing is that we ask Roland where the duchess's daughter was buried so we can lay her mother's bones to rest near her," Jay stated.

"Jay, I've called the coroner to come collect the bones," the sheriff informed him.

"Is that her skull?' Susan asked, pointing to something protruding out of the wall.

"I believe so," Jay confirmed. "If the jewels hadn't been with her, we wouldn't have known it was the duchess. It could have been anyone that wandered the property and fell into the well."

"This is a historic find. No one ever knew what happened to Duchess Sophia and her daughter and now they will," Susan stated.

"Better than that," Jay started. "A mother and daughter have been reunited after over a hundred years of being apart, and their spirits can move on together now."

"You're such a romantic," Susan teased.

"Yeah, I guess I am." He chuckled. "Shall we go show these to my mom?"

The crowd gathered close to Jay and Susan as they showed the emerald pieces to Martha. Phil Cook was among the bystanders. He apologized profusely to Jay for his clerk leaking the story. She had since been fired because, in the jewelry business, trust plays a big part in the client's confidence to use your services.

"I would love to appraise the collection," Phil offered.

"That would be fine, but I have to research the legalities of finding a treasure of this magnitude. I will be in touch," Jay promised the jeweler.

The coroner's wagon arrived to take over the dig. They would bring the bones to the coroner's office where they would see if they could extract DNA for testing. Later, the bones would be released for burial.

"Come on, Jay. I'll escort you and that treasure home safely," the sheriff offered.

Susan and Martha returned to the cottage with Jay. He left the others outside while he went inside and placed the emeralds into his secret safe. The others joined him moments later.

"This calls for a celebration," Martha said, grabbing a bottle of champagne out of the wine refrigerator in the kitchen.

She poured everyone a glass and then toasted her son and Roland for being such a smart ghost. At the mention of his name, he shimmered into the living room.

Jay... Come with me.

He floated through the kitchen and through the back door that led out to the point. Jay followed while the others watched from the bay window inside the cottage. Jay and the ghost stood out in the sea grass as if waiting for something.

"Look!" Martha exclaimed.

Two other figures had joined Jay and Roland—an older looking woman that no one had ever seen before and the young ghost of Colleen. They talked for several minutes. The two female ghosts joined hands and walked off the edge of the point together and vanished. Roland disappeared next, and Jay turned to walk back to the house.

"Well? What did they say?" Martha asked all excited.

"They were grateful for all the help. Their spirits moved on together. I don't think we will be seeing Colleen's ghost out on the point anymore," Jay replied.

Roland appeared in the corner of the room. He was smiling.

"I hope this brings you a little bit of peace, my friend, knowing that you never would have found the body of Colleen's mother no matter how hard you looked," Jay said. "And she didn't blame you at all for the wreck of the ship. She said it was so bad out on the water that they wouldn't have seen the lighthouse's beam through the storm."

I am happy for Colleen... She has found her mother.

"You did it, Roland. You do have to show me where you buried Colleen's body so we can bury her mother with her," Jay informed the ghost.

Can't... It's been taken by the ocean.

"Maybe you can cremate Duchess Sophia's bones and spread them over the ocean to join her daughter," Susan suggested.

They are already joined... forever.

Roland faded out of sight, and the others stood there in silence thinking about what the ghost had said. It didn't really matter about the bones that had been found. Their souls had already moved on.

"I don't know about anyone else, but I'm starving. How about we fire up the grill and make a celebratory meal, one fit for a duchess? And Christmas is only one week away, and my tree is still sitting on the back porch," Jay stated. "Who wants to help decorate my tree?"

Martha walked over to her son and hugged him.

"I am so proud of you. You did a great thing here today," she praised him.

"The praise should go to Roland."

"I will tell him later, but if you hadn't followed through, a mother and daughter might not be in heaven tonight, reunited," Martha replied. "Did you ever find out how the comb got into the tunnel below the café?"

"I asked the duchess about that. She had given a man the comb as payment to help search for her daughter. That was how it came to be separated from the rest of the collection," Jay explained. "She doesn't know how it got in the tunnel."

"Fate. That's how it ended up there. You were supposed to find it to help them move on," Martha surmised. "And speaking of fate, how are you and Susan getting along?"

"You will never give up, will you, Mom?"

"Not as long as I have no grandchildren." She laughed.

"Someday, you will," Jay answered, smiling fondly at Susan.

RECIPES

CLAM FRITTERS

1 egg well beaten

¾ cup of strained clam juice

(liquid drained from clams or bottled clam juice)

3 tablespoons vegetable oil

¼ cup milk

1 cup of finely chopped clams

1/2 teaspoon salt (to taste)

2 teaspoons baking powder

1 ½ cups of all-purpose flour

Extra oil for frying

Combine wet ingredients in a bowl and whisk together. (not the minced clams)

In another bowl, combine the dry ingredients and then whisk in the egg mixture. Fold in minced clams. The batter should be the consistency of a thick cake batter.

Heat about 2 inches of vegetable oil in a deep skillet to about 370 degrees.

Drop rounded tablespoons of batter into oil for frying, cooking each side for 2 to 3 minutes until puffy and golden brown.

Place on paper towel to drain excess oil.

Serve hot with fresh lemon slices or hot sauce.

Makes about 2 to 3 dozen fritters depending on the size when cooked.

CREOLE FLOUNDER

4 medium tomatoes, chopped

2 cloves of fresh garlic

1 cup chopped green pepper

1 cup chopped onion

3 pounds fresh flounder filets

Preheat oven to 375 degrees

Mix the first four ingredients in a saucepan and simmer about 15 minutes or until tender.

Place the fish in a shallow buttered baking dish in a single layer.

Pour the sauce mixture over the fish and bake for 25 minutes.

Serve with rice.

CRAB TOAST ROUNDS

Party appetizer

1 ½ sticks of butter or margarine

Freshly ground pepper

1 teaspoon nutmeg

3 pounds of lump crabmeat

Two tablespoons of brandy

¼ cup of chopped parsley

12 slices of bread

Melt butter in large skillet. Add pepper (to taste), nutmeg, crabmeat, brandy, and parsley. Sauté over low heat for about 5 minutes.

While mixture is cooking, use the rim of any glass to cut out circles from the center of the bread slices. Place on cookie sheet and lightly brown each side under the broiler.

Place crab meat mixture in the center of a serving dish and surround it with the toasted rounds.

Garnish with lemons and more fresh parsley.

Made in the USA
Middletown, DE
24 April 2020

91622397R00087